FAKING IT

KAIT GAMBLE

Dedication

For the Jane Bonds out there.

Books by Kait Gamble

The Long Way Round

Grind
Ignite
Scorch

Lust Bites

Cuffed

Sexy Snax

Blind Spot

Totally Five Star

Breaking Rossi's Rules
Fuel to the Fire
Sins in the Sand
Faking It

Single Titles

Weathering the Storm

Faking It

ISBN # 978-1-78686-103-0

©Copyright Kait Gamble 2016

Cover Art by Posh Gosh ©Copyright 2016

Interior text design by Claire Siemaszkiewicz

Totally Bound Publishing

Published in 2016 by Totally Bound Publishing, Newland House, The Point, Weaver Road, Lincoln, LN6 3QN, United Kingdom.

Chapter One

With Valentino caressing her body, Louboutin gracing her feet and Bulgari glittering from her ears, neck and wrists, Ana strode into the grand ballroom of the Totally Five Star Chamonix. The envy and admiration in the eyes of all who turned to gaze at her were almost palpable, despite the other women wearing couture of the same caliber.

Under the arching intricately veneered wood ceiling, Ana waded through the throng, eyes sharp, head held high. The fine fabric of her deep-red gown swished decadently around her legs as she moved. Though it was nearing Christmas, she had chosen a dress that left her arms, shoulders and most of her back bare. The anxiety and excitement of simply being there were enough to blast any and all discomfort away.

It had been a long time since she'd been in any room dressed as she was. Even longer since she'd been in a room with people who exuded this much wealth. Ana could almost smell it in the air. But then she'd always had a good nose when it came to finding money.

She had to take a moment, however, to just take in the amazing ballroom. She didn't know where to look first. From the gleaming floor to the vaulted ceiling, complicated designs were played out with inlaid wood. Plush red-velvet curtains tied back with braids of gold decorated the massive multi-paned windows. Three golden chandeliers lit the room from above while man-sized floor candelabras provided pools of light strategically around the room.

It was as if she'd walked into a fairy tale.

As calm and nonchalant as she might have appeared, Ana had already started scanning the gloriously opulent room the instant the doors parted, automatically appraising and separating the genuine from the fake. Even with the number of imitations she saw, there was enough real glitter to cause her knees to weaken a little.

Her pulse sped up to a gallop and her palms grew slick. It wasn't fear. It wasn't that she felt out of her depth. It was the adrenaline. The excitement coursed through her. Something that hadn't happened in a very long time.

Ana clamped down on her impulse to liberate a few of the glittering beauties as she walked past.

"Anastasia? Is that you?"

The lilting Irish voice drew her attention. As did the use of the name of a long dormant identity.

Ana put on a big smile and turned on her heel to face the willowy brunette gaping at her in delighted amazement. "Ciara, how lovely to see you."

"I'm astonished to see *you*. You haven't been out and about in far too long." Ciara grasped Ana by the shoulders and air-kissed her, bringing with her a cloud of perfume that reminded Ana of exotic night-blooming flowers. "We all thought you'd dropped off the earth."

In a way, she had. Not that she was about to share the reason with anyone. "I've been busy. You know what it's like when you're on the charity circuit."

"But I haven't seen you at any of the events. We were really beginning to wonder." Curiosity and speculation were clear in her big blue eyes as she swept her gaze over Ana again. It was just like her to take in every detail in order to better relay the meeting later to the 'we' she'd mentioned. The close-knit group of women who used them as much to gather gossip as to help.

They were obviously very concerned about her disappearance since no one called or ever bothered to even email her. There hadn't been so much as a text. Not that it mattered. If they *had* approached her, it would have only been to sate their curiosity more than any true concern about her well-being.

It made her glad that this world wasn't the one she truly belonged in.

Ana shrugged. "I've been working behind the scenes." As if that explained everything.

Ciara nodded sagely. "I see. Tired of the limelight?"

"You could say that." Ana swept her gaze around the room. "So who's all here?"

The tall brunette linked her arm with Ana's and started a slow promenade into the crowd. "Everyone who's anyone, darling. It's the Winter Ball, and no one misses it."

She vaguely wondered what the crowd thought of her having missed the last two. The extravagant affair happened every year, acting like a homing beacon for the rich and famous who had time and money to splash out from Christmas Eve to New Year's Day.

It had also become a smorgasbord for the discerning singles looking for that special, very wealthy someone.

Ana made sure her smile was predatory as she took in the attendees. "That, I gathered. Anyone new and noteworthy?" Those would be the ones Ana needed to know about.

Ciara's tinkling laugh drew gazes from around them. "On the prowl?"

"I might be." Ana could only imagine her reaction if she knew the truth.

A knowing smile on her face, Ciara nodded. "I should have known. You wouldn't have shown up looking so fabulous in a dress like that without an ulterior motive. Unless it's to make the old biddies choke on their tongues."

She turned Ana around and pointed into the crowd at a group that were listening avidly to a story being told by a rather animated man whose stomach rolled and bounced with every wave of his arms.

"That's JJ or AJ...or something." Ciara waved away his last name as if it meant nothing. "Some upstart from Texas. More money than God, but less personality than a gnat. Says he's going to revolutionize...something. To be honest, I stopped listening about three seconds into the conversation. The halitosis…" She groaned. "He's no one's type. Moving on…"

Ciara scanned the room with her vivid blue eyes until they landed on her next target. She nodded at the tall, leggy blonde who could have passed for a supermodel. "That's Arabella Ignatius. She's the daughter of Hendrik Ignatius, the Norwegian industrialist. She's just come into her trust and is spending it as fast as she can. Rumor has it most of it is going up her nose while the rest is wasted on a string of men and trinkets for them. And when I say trinkets, I'm talking about cars, plastic surgery and holidays abroad."

Lovely. A blowhard and a girl who thought love could be bought. Ana had no interest in either of them. They weren't who she was here for. "I can't say I'm looking forward to meeting them."

"Then don't. There are a few more." She pointed at a group of young men deep in conversation. "Some new pups with even newer money." Then she steered her to look at another group swilling champagne. "And the usual penniless aristos playacting as if they've still got a few coins left."

She paused in her sweep of the room and a smirk spread over her lips. "There's the mysterious Mr. Cabral who, between you and me, stinks of cartel money." She jerked her head toward a swarthy man with a roguish smile who had a veritable harem surrounding him. "If you want to take a run at him, you'd better get a head start to get through that."

Ana definitely took note of him, not because of his looks, but because of the vibe she got from him. He was dangerous.

She averted her gaze before he could sense her attention on him.

"Oh! And over there!" Ciara turned Ana around and pointed into the crowd at a tall, broad and darkly handsome man. "That's Armand Cassells. He's that famous chef from the Caribbean, if you remember. He's taken over as director of dining and entertainment for the Totally Five Star. I think that's the mighty Claudia Bauer with him now."

Everyone knew who Claudia Bauer was. The dragon guarding the gates to the CEO of Totally Five Star Hotels himself, James Conroy III. If anyone wanted to see him, they had to get through her first. Ana vaguely wondered if the CEO was making an appearance for the ball this year.

"And I have to introduce you to my date." Ciara grinned as she searched the room. "He's gone off to get drinks. I think you'll like him. You're into the tall, dark and handsome types, aren't you?"

And there was the catty Ciara Ana remembered. The one who loved to gloat and lord her prizes over everyone else.

Ana shrugged. She might have been into the tall, dark and handsome type of man before, but she was no longer interested in wasting time with any. She had found the love of her life once and had lost him far too soon. No one would replace him.

Her heart throbbed as she thought back to the gorgeous, romantic man and the blissful few months they'd had together before tragedy struck. She hated to remember it, hated that it had happened, but she had to remember that it had all turned out okay.

Ciara's voice tore through her morose thoughts.

"Are you all right?" Ciara's smug expression turned into concern. "You look as if you're going to be ill."

"I'm fine." Swallowing the emotions, Ana patted her friend's arm. The pain that came from remembering had lessened over the past couple of years, but she doubted it would ever go away.

"If you're sure." She gave her one last look before returning her gaze to the crowd. "He's quite wealthy on top of being drop-dead gorgeous. Wickedly smart, as well."

Clenching her teeth, Ana mustered the strength to meet Ciara's latest fling then she needed to get moving. A smile, a few pleasantries, then she was done. The sooner she could get away, the sooner she could get out of there and back to her quiet life.

"Ciara, there you are."

The man who approached certainly was tall, dark and handsome but there was something about him that came across as less than refined. The smarmy glint in his eyes, as they lingered on her breasts and exposed skin, made Ana want to take a shower.

"Estefan, I'd like to introduce you to Countess Anastasia Deveaux. Ana, this is my Estefan."

He took her hand and brushed his lips over her knuckles. Ana made a mental note to bathe it in hand sanitizer.

"Estefan Rocha. It is always a pleasure to meet one of Ciara's friends. Especially one so beautiful."

Ana nodded. "Charmed." She couldn't be less so. Ana didn't recognize his name. He was more than likely the typical playboy type who showed up to occasions like this in hopes of landing a wealthy socialite like Ciara.

The kind of man she despised.

Unfortunately, Ciara seemed totally taken with him.

Ana smiled politely. It wasn't any of her business.

He went on about something that Ana couldn't have cared less about. Watching Ciara fawn over him like a lovesick puppy rolled her stomach so much that Ana was sure that her cheeks were beginning to tinge green.

She let her gaze wander every now and again, hoping the hint that she was losing interest would be picked up, but neither seemed to notice her inattention and continued to regale her with the tale of the time they were in Majorca and saw a turtle.

A goddamned turtle.

It was on the eighteenth or so time that she looked away that her gaze was snared by Cabral across the room. Even someone that made her skin crawl as he did was preferable to listening to Ciara simper and giggle any longer.

She gave him a coy half-smile that was enough to have him cleave a path across the room toward her.

He was good-looking, but he had an aura of danger. Menace. The closer he got, the more Ana agreed with

Ciara's initial assessment. He held himself with smarmy self-confidence. That, coupled with the scar she detected on his neck that disappeared into the open collar of his shirt, told her this was a man who had known violence. Might have even incited it.

Ciara's scandalized gasp when he swept in mid-sentence, took Ana's hand and kissed it was loud enough to draw even more attention than he already had by abandoning his little circle of admirers.

"Diego Cabral." He kissed her hand. "I apologize for intruding, but I couldn't help myself. I can't recall ever seeing you around before. Surely, I would have remembered one as beautiful as you."

"This is *Countess* Anastasia Deveaux." Ciara had puffed up with indignation at his overfamiliarity with Ana. "You will treat her with the proper respect."

The title sparked more interest in Cabral's dark eyes. "A countess. How fascinating. Come, you can tell me all about your undoubtedly exciting life over drinks."

"Ana…" Ciara's whisper had a warning tone to it.

"I'll be fine. We must catch up again soon." Ana linked her arm through the one Cabral offered. "Nice to meet you, Estefan."

They were well out of earshot when her new companion broke the silence. "I hope you don't mind me taking you away from your friends."

Ana had to chuckle. "Not at all. I was losing interest in their inane travel stories. Anyway, I think I've found someone much more interesting." She almost gagged saying the words, but she knew he would be more than likely to lead her to what she sought.

He led her farther into the crowd and waved over a waiter carrying a tray glittering with champagne flutes. Retrieving a couple, he handed her one, tapping the rim of his with hers as he did. "*Salud.*"

Ana kept the smile stiff on her lips as she took a tiny sip.

"So, a *countess*. I'm fascinated already."

"I'm not that interesting, I assure you. Just your run-of-the-mill titled lady."

He chuckled as he let his gaze wander over her. "Titled, perhaps, but run-of-the-mill? Never."

If he only knew…

Ana listened to his banal chitchat. Most of it was boastful. All of it was about himself. She couldn't imagine having to spend more than a few minutes with someone like him.

She caught glimpses of what was going on around them while he talked. Ana did her best not to make it too obvious, but when he launched into a tale about how he had blown a tire and had changed it by himself, Ana had reached her limit.

"So, Mr. Cabral, I can't imagine I'm the most interesting person you've met at this party."

He studied her with a calculating gaze. "Fishing for compliments, or are you truly interested?"

"Interested, of course. I've missed the past few events and am curious to see who's popped up on the radar."

Cabral nodded. "Keeping tabs on any upstarts — I love it. Very wise." He swept his gaze around the room contemplatively. "You wouldn't be worried by any of the young ones, I'm sure. None have any of your charm."

Ana took a long, slow breath, wanting him to just get on with it. She disguised it with a sip from her drink.

"There are a couple of new faces I met earlier. The man was forgettable enough, but the woman… Beautiful, yes, but far too intellectual for my liking."

Because, presumably, he preferred his women large-breasted and only smart enough to draw air regularly.

Ana forced a smile. "She sounds intriguing."

"She's duller than dust." Cabral gazed at her critically. "You're not seriously interested in talking to the woman."

"Why wouldn't I be?" Ana smirked when his face fell. It had finally dawned on him that she wasn't as dim-witted as he'd hoped and he had little chance of bedding a countess that night. Ana smiled charmingly and placed a hand on his arm. "Please, introduce us?"

Muttering something under his breath, he led her through the crowd. It didn't take long before it was clear that they were headed for a voluptuous redhead in a skin-tight golden gown.

She turned to smile in recognition at Cabral, nearly dislodging her barely captured breasts at the same time.

"Mr. Cabral! How nice to see you again." She shook his hand before turning her gaze to Ana. "I don't think we've met."

"Christine Nowak, I'd like you to meet Countess Anastasia Deveaux."

Her honey-colored eyes widened at the title. "A countess! How exciting! Should I bow or something?"

Ana shook her head. "It's a pleasure."

She toyed with a tendril of her fiery hair. "I'm just really excited to be here, you know? I've already met more millionaires and billionaires tonight than I thought existed on the planet. And so many models and heiresses. Whew!" Christine fanned her cheeks as she reined herself in. "This isn't something I do on a regular basis. Obviously."

"Oh?" Ana leaned in. "What is it that you do?"

A proud smile lit up her face. "I'm a gemologist."

Ana smiled in earnest for the first time that night. "How fascinating. Gems are among some of my favorite things."

"Mine too."

Cabral laughed gruffly. "Two women who love sparkling gemstones. Never would have expected that."

"You know what they say about women and diamonds," Ana purred. She ran her fingers over the glittering specimens at her neck. "So, Christine, what brings you out tonight? I assume it must be a special occasion since it's not something you do very often."

Ana hadn't thought it possible, but the woman's face lit up even more.

"I'm here for the exhibition. I'm representing Claiborne Diamonds."

"How exciting." Ana's palms grew slick at the thought of all the gems simply waiting to be plucked—but she *had* to focus. "You'll have to show me around the exhibits. An expert eye like yours would be invaluable."

"Of course! I would be honored to." Christine bounced a little, nearly vaulting her unruly chest out of the bodice of her dress. Cabral definitely seemed more interested in her now. "I do have a date. He's gone off somewhere getting us drinks, but I'm sure he won't mind if you join us." She turned to Cabral, obviously thinking he was Ana's date.

"The more the merrier, I always say." The man next to her obviously had more than the exhibition in mind.

Ana ignored him, shrugging his arm off her when he went to wind it around her shoulders. "You don't have to accompany us, Mr. Cabral. I'm sure you have other people you have to see before the night ends. Besides, it will be rather boring with us gushing over jewelry."

"Not at all. It might give me some ideas on what to get as a gift for my next special someone." He winked almost lasciviously.

As if the hint of the possibility of him buying her something outrageously expensive would turn her head. If he knew the worth of the gems she had held in her hands in her lifetime, his head would spin.

Ana shrugged. "Suit yourself." She linked her arm through Christine's—who had been watching, enraptured by the interplay—and started walking. "Shall we take a look, then?"

"But my date…"

"Will find you," Ana cooed. "A gorgeous woman like you stands out. If he's smart, he'll make it back before someone else steps into his place."

Christine giggled, turning a bright shade of pink at the blatant flattery. "I hardly stand out. Not compared to you."

Was she kidding? Her breasts alone were causing eyes to bug all around them. "Oh, you do. That hair. That dress. Anyone who lets you think that you belong in the background is a fool."

Cabral, now forgotten, trailed behind like a lost puppy as they wandered through the crowd into an anteroom and soon disappeared into the crowd.

Not that Ana cared.

Focused now on the job, Ana's attention went straight to the glass boxes of various sizes that stood on lit pedestals displaying their treasures.

Ana's pulse roared in her ears. A rainbow of gems in a myriad of sizes winked teasingly at her from their displays, some mounted in dazzling settings, others loose and begging her to snatch them up. Diamonds sparkled icily. Grass-green emeralds, warm amethysts, cool sapphires and red-hot rubies winked provocatively from their prisons. Uncut. Cut into glittering shapes. Necklaces. Rings. Earrings. Tiaras. Even belly chains and anklets. Everything imaginable was there to tempt and tease. It was a stunning display and almost too much for Ana's senses to handle.

Overloaded, she dumbly let Christine lead her to the closest display, though she barely heard a thing the woman said as she described the gems and shared little anecdotes about them.

All of Ana's senses were attuned to what was enclosed on the other side of the glass. Her first instinct was to look for vulnerabilities, security flaws…

She snapped herself out of it and turned her focus to the woman still prattling on about carats and inclusions, nothing that Ana couldn't already see herself. But she let Christine talk. In her experience, the more people talked, the more relaxed and confident they became. And that was exactly what Ana wanted to happen so she could pump her for more information.

"…and that's how they found this beauty." Christine pointed at the emerald the size of both Ana's fists pressed together.

"How fascinating." There wasn't a gem in the room that Ana didn't already know every detail about, thanks to the boasting the event planners had done online. Color, weight, clarity, even the sponsors of each display had been gleefully shared. All it had taken was a few minutes of reading on the flight over. But, it had all been superfluous information in her mind.

What she was looking for was one diamond in particular... Where was it?

"Are you interested in certain gems? I'm sure there's something here that will capture your fancy." Christine smiled expectantly.

Ana pretended to think about it a moment. "I'm into diamonds. The bigger the better."

Christine's grin grew. "Who doesn't think that?" She winked. "I do believe I know of one that will stun you. Follow me."

She led Ana through the thick crowd of people toward a display case near the center of the room.

Now that was more like it. Ana stepped as close as she could without pressing her nose against the glass. "It's incredible."

"It is." Christine smiled almost proudly as she gazed at it. "Three hundred carats, nearly flawless, almost completely colorless..." She sighed wistfully.

"What I could do with that." Ana knew that she seemed as though she was looking at the gem covetously, and she was, up to a point, but, in truth, she was assessing the diamond, its case and the security warding it.

"It's big enough to do just about anything with, but I think cutting it would be such a waste. Something that magnificent would need to stay intact."

"It would make a stellar knuckle duster."

Christine chortled gleefully. "That it would."

The redhead seemed quite happy to let Ana stand and stare and even joined her in companionable silence. Their quiet regard of the stone was interrupted too soon.

"Christine, I thought I would find you here."

The confident, urbane British-accented voice came from

behind them. For a moment, Ana thought she had imagined the voice that still haunted her dreams. But when she turned, she wondered if she might be dreaming after all.

Ciara hadn't been lying when she said her type was tall, dark and handsome. This man fit the description.

Exactly so.

The world turned into a fuzzy haze while the noise filtered away to a droning hum, as if her mind barely had the capacity to focus on the man and the powerful impact simply seeing him again had on her. And the memories that came flooding back when their gazes met.

There was no doubt about who he was. Rhys was still tall and rangy, but his dark hair was shorter, the clipped accent was a far cry from the husky whispers she could recall and he was in a crisp tuxedo rather than a ratty T-shirt and jeans, but it was definitely the man she remembered. Had longed for. Dreamed about.

Rhys Stone.

She reached out to touch him. Needing to determine that this wasn't a hallucination.

The man she loved. A man she'd seen die…

Rhys' smile faltered as did his feet when he saw her, but he quickly regained his equilibrium and handed his drink to Christine with a smile before casually winding his arm around her waist. The stunned expression on Ana's beautiful face as her arm dropped to her side mirrored what clawed at his insides.

Ana Meier.

Her shock was quickly hidden behind a hard, icy façade. He wasn't prepared for how quickly she seemed able to shutter herself off to him. Not when he wanted — expected — to see at least a little joy at seeing him again.

Rhys wasn't quite able to do the same, at least not inwardly. As he kept the polite smile on his face, his hands itched to touch the one whom he'd been dreaming about seeing again for two seemingly endless years. God, she was still as beautiful as he remembered. Curvy, long-limbed, sloe-eyed and tumbling waves of chestnut hair all put together in a combination that made his mouth water and other parts of his anatomy throb.

What was she doing here? And showing enough skin to turn the head of more than one man. Rhys fought back the impulse to cover her with his jacket...as well as run his hands — his mouth — over every inch of flesh that was exposed.

Christine said something and touched his arm to gain his attention. "Richard, I'd like you to meet Countess Anastasia Deveaux. I was just giving her a guided tour of the exhibition."

Ana smiled tightly at him, ignoring his outstretched hand. If the angry glint in her eyes had anything to say about things, she wasn't pleased to see him. In fact, she looked as though she was done having anything to do with him and wanted to get as far away as possible.

"Charmed to meet you, *Richard*."

The way she practically snarled the name might as well have been an ice pick to the gut. He continued to smile, however. "I don't think I've ever met a countess before."

And he still hadn't. Rhys was sure of that much. The way she closed herself off so quickly and the fact that Ana hadn't even flinched when Christine used his alias led him to think that there was a lot more to her than she had let on during their all too brief romance.

She looked around expectantly, causing Rhys' gut to tighten in response.

Was she here with someone else? Had she found someone else? Was that so farfetched? Ana was a beautiful, vibrant woman. Who in their right mind would give up the chance to be with her?

And that body...

He was well aware that he'd been staring too long and too hard. It was impossible not to. The combination of her curves and that dress were enough to have his blood flowing south. Rhys had to forcibly stop himself from reaching out and touching skin that he knew would be silky-soft under his hand. Or kissing those lips…

How could she walk in there looking like that, wearing that dress, and expect every man in the room with eyes not to notice her?

Did she dress that way for a man? Was she here to snare one? Or was that what her new man liked? To flaunt her like some trophy? Where was the bastard? Rhys itched to take him down a peg or two.

Still staring daggers at him, Ana sniffed disdainfully. "It was nice talking to you, Christine." She slid her icy gaze to him. "Richard."

As if the cold growl was any way to say goodbye. Rhys would make sure that they would see each other again. And soon. "It was my most sincere pleasure meeting you, Countess."

She barely spared him a parting glance before turning and disappearing into the crowd.

"Do you know her?" Christine asked.

Rhys continued to stare at the spot where she had melted into the throng. "I really don't."

Robotically making her way through the room, Ana kept her back ramrod straight in an attempt to keep from falling over. Rhys…Richard…whoever he was…was alive and well and apparently dating scientists and attending parties as if nothing had happened.

He remembered her clearly as well as she did him. Ana had seen it in his eyes. So what was he playing at?

Head reeling, she looked for somewhere quiet so she could gather her wits—or throw up. Not much chance of either in the ballroom with an eponymous ball in full swing. Yet the thought of going back up to her room didn't hold appeal.

The need to do what she was meant to and get out of there was infinitely more insistent now.

What was he? A con? A cop? More importantly, *who* was he? He was clearly going by an alias at this party. Or did that mean he had lied to her about who he was before? Was everything that had happened between them a lie? But the most important question was would he be a problem?

Definitely not.

Ana shoved aside the emotions threatening to swamp her. Sadness, betrayal…they were all swiftly locked away deep inside. She would have time to deal with them later.

At least Ana hoped she would have that luxury.

She couldn't afford anything to derail her. Not this time. There was too much at stake.

Taking a moment to center herself, Ana turned her gaze back to the room and the people filling it.

Not that she took anything in. Her head reeled with what had just happened. Rhys? Rhys was alive and here? How could that be? What had happened to him? Why hadn't he tried to contact her? Had he faked his own death to get away from her? Had things been getting too serious too quickly for him? Or had she been getting too close to finding out the truth about him?

It was all so crazy, but not as mind-boggling as him coming back to life.

It was too much to deal with and she didn't have the indulgence of time. Ana shoved all the questions deep down with the roiling emotions. Once she was out of there, she could break down or whatever she needed to get over it. But right now, it was imperative to keep her head in the game.

Taking a deep breath, Ana straightened her shoulders and fixed a tranquil expression on her face. She knew what she was after and where to find it. She merely had to get it, and this whole thing could be put behind her.

Then she could get on with her life once more.

Chapter Two

Rhys strolled down the quiet corridor knowing that his every move was being recorded by the near invisible sentinels tucked discreetly at the corners. He headed straight for the door numbered eight twenty-six, tapped the key card he had ready in his hand to the reader and quietly pushed the door open.

Silence. Which was to be expected at two a.m.

He quietly closed the door behind him and silently padded farther into the room. While much smaller, Ana's suite was well decorated and spacious enough that it didn't feel like a hotel room. Exactly what was expected of a hotel under the Totally Five Star banner.

Rhys made his way through the living area, the kitchen, stuck his head in the various rooms as he passed, but after the quick look-around, he found it unpredictably empty.

Where was she?

The knot in his gut tightened at the myriad of ideas for reasons why she wouldn't be there. He steeled himself against them. Better that she wasn't there. It would give him a chance to investigate more thoroughly.

The rooms were exceptionally tidy, as if she hadn't spent time in there at all. If she had, she had become insanely organized. She hadn't seemed particularly bothered by a little mess when they were together before. Then again, they hadn't been interested with anything more than getting naked during that time.

Whatever the reason, it made his job easier. Rhys strode into the bedroom to find that it was just as tidy as the other rooms. The sole indication that there was anyone even staying there was a duffel bag next to the bed.

Intrigued, he unzipped the leather bag and took a quick look inside. Nothing out of the ordinary. An assortment of clothing, shoes, boots, a bag filled with toiletries and – a steel reinforced rope with collapsible grappling hook?

Startled, Rhys stood and took half a step back. What the hell? Why would she need climbing gear? He could understand if it was for exploring the terrain around the hotel, but this was specialist equipment meant for indoor use...

Questioning if he was in the right room now, Rhys ran his hands through his hair as he knelt once again to close the bag before he moved on to the closet.

And was kicked in the back.

Pain flared from the point of impact and again when his head slammed into the wall. Head reeling, he twisted, narrowly missing a kick to the head. Letting instinct take over, he stayed low and lunged for his assailant's knees, knocking the newcomer off balance and sending them to the floor. Hard.

He would have punched the attacker in the face, but checked himself when the grunt that came out of the person he'd knocked down made it clear that he was fighting a woman. The scent and the body he felt under the clothes told him he knew this woman well.

She kneed him solidly in the ribs then rolled to stand in the moonlight streaming in through the windows.

Her dark hair hung in loose waves over her shoulders and the shadow it created obscured her features, but Rhys would know her anywhere.

He put up his hands. "Ana, it's me. Rhys."

"I know," she snarled before nailing him with a side kick in the gut.

She knocked the wind from him, but confusion trumped the pain. He straightened and fended off her other blows. It took him a second to find his opening. He lunged, grabbing her arms and twisting them behind her.

Ana let out a sound of pure frustration as she struggled. As she did, the delicious scent of her wound itself around him, reminding him of warm summer days and even hotter nights. The memories, the feel of her against him, twisted his insides into knots.

"Relax."

Ana fought him stubbornly. Had she always been this strong?

She growled something as an overture to stomping on his foot and twisting, dropping her shoulder and ramming him into the wall again.

Ana flipped her hair out of her face and glared at him, clearly ready to take him down again if she needed to. "What are you doing here, Rhys? If that's even your real name."

He grabbed her again and pinned her arm behind her back. "Of course it is." Rhys didn't get the other arm fast enough, and she swung. He narrowly deflected a back fist aimed at his face and secured her arm with the other. "Jesus, Ana, will you please calm down?"

"Not until you tell me what you're doing here. *Alive.*" He caught the hitch in her voice and something in his chest fractured. "You died. I saw you die."

Pain ripped through him at seeing hers. "Ana…"

"Get out." The raw anguish in her eyes cut him to the quick.

He put up his hands. "Not until we talk."

"There's nothing to talk about." She dropped her arms, but her eyes never wavered from him. "Security are probably on their way up. You should leave."

Did he want to have to explain himself to security? Rhys brushed the lump growing on his crown. He hissed at the sting and the warm sticky wetness that could only be blood. He wasn't sure if he was pissed off or impressed. "I can deal with them."

"And tell them what? That you just happened to wander into the wrong locked room at this time of night?"

23

He shrugged. There were plenty of explanations they could use. "It's not unheard of for men and women to migrate to different hotel rooms in the middle of the night."

There was a glint of anger flashing in her eyes. "Get out, Rhys."

"We need to talk."

"We really don't." As angry and as in control as she seemed to be, Ana visibly jumped when there was a knock at the door. Pointing at his feet, she growled, "Stand there and stay quiet."

Ana dashed from the room and, moments later, her voice took on a pleading tone as she tried to placate whoever it was at the door. Though it sounded as if she was having a little trouble convincing them that nothing was going on.

Rhys tossed the bed and took off his shirt on the way to the en suite bathroom. Seconds later, he reemerged in a towel an instant before the security guard and Ana walked in.

"Sorry, did we disturb our neighbors?" He switched on the light and pressed his palm to his head to show him the blood. "I'm such a klutz. I came down to surprise my girl and sneaking around in the dark wasn't exactly the best idea. Obviously. And, well..." Rhys shrugged and let the man fill in the rest of the story himself.

"Right." The bulldog of a man looked a little skeptical but slowly nodded as his gaze bounced between them. "Would you like me to call for a doctor to tend to your wound?"

Rhys kept the sheepish grin on his face. "No, it's all right. We've already taken enough of your time. I'm sure my darling Ana can help me out." He gazed at her lovingly and was mildly surprised that she didn't try to scratch his eyes out.

The security guard grumbled something that sounded like agreement as he shrugged. "Just try to be quiet, *ça va*? No more sneaking around."

Appearing as contrite as he could manage, Rhys smirked. "Of course. So sorry for disturbing you."

Ana followed the man out but not before giving him a deadly glare.

What? He had gotten the man out of there, hadn't he? And with no questions asked. He chalked it up as a win. What did she have to be so angry about?

He listened while she bade the man goodnight and promised not to make any more noise.

Moments later, she strode back into the room. "He's gone. Now get out."

"Not even a thank you?" Rhys noticed that she kept her eyes strictly above the neckline. Interesting.

She crossed her arms tightly over her chest. "For what? Causing him to come up and investigate in the first place?"

"For getting rid of him without having to answer a bunch of needless questions." He lifted his shoulders, which had the added bonus of dropping the towel a little. "You're welcome."

Her gaze flicked down for a fraction of a second. "I didn't thank you."

Rhys caught the way her pupils dilated when she swept her attention over him and allowed himself a small smile. "You're welcome just the same."

Interest piqued by the color in her cheeks, he simply stood there tempting her to look again.

And she did several times before she visibly regained her anger and allowed it to quickly suffuse her beautiful body once more. She wore it like armor against him. But why? Seeing her again was a pleasant coincidence. Sure, she might have thought he was dead, a minor detail, but now that they were face to face, what was there to stop them from at least talking and giving him the chance to explain?

He had to admit to himself that he wanted to do more than talk. A hell of a lot more. Even with her glaring daggers at him, his mind raced with all kinds of X-rated scenarios about how he could change that. Rhys knew he had to get her hackles down before anything else could feasibly happen. It was going to be hard to even get her to listen to him at the moment.

"I know it must be a huge shock seeing me. I can't say that seeing you here isn't a surprise to me, too, but can we talk like two adults? Don't we owe each other that much?"

"I owe you nothing."

Her voice reminded him of the winter winds blasting outside. Could he blame her? "Right. I guess that's all there is to be said, then."

Rhys looked around and grabbed his clothes. He tugged them on with quick, impatient moves.

"When you're ready to talk, come find me. I'm in the penthouse."

Rhys stalked out of the door.

Ana willed her heart to slow. Not easy after all that. Allowing herself a moment to settle back into some semblance of normal, she tried to wrap her head around what had just happened.

Rhys had been in her room. For what? To snoop? To find her? For more? To show up at two a.m. would mean he expected her to be there. So what had he done when he found she wasn't? How long had he been snooping around the suite? She cursed herself for not taking precautions and securing the suite properly. Her mind was more scattered than she would like to admit.

There wasn't much for him to rifle through at least. Ana hadn't had time to pack properly. She had grabbed a few essentials then immediately flown in to get the job done. Something which she had planned on doing that very night except there had been an unexpected hitch. She hadn't been alone in the gallery where the jewels were on show.

Ana hadn't seen anyone, but she knew there had been another person. Someone lurking in the shadows. She had been sure of it. They were careful, whoever they were, but Ana had a sixth sense about that sort of thing. Within a few minutes of sneaking in, she knew someone was watching her. So before even making an attempt on anything, Ana had gotten the hell out of there only to find someone else in her room.

Already on edge, of course she was going to go on the attack. Then to find it was Rhys who was in her suite, uninvited, and most definitely unwanted, the cold edge of trepidation had turned into white-hot rage. How dare he show up and wander into her suite as if he belonged there!

As if he hadn't abandoned her for the past two years. As if he hadn't already torn her heart out by letting her believe he was dead.

And he wanted to talk? Just brush everything aside like he had done nothing more than missed a coffee date? It incensed her further to think that if they hadn't come face-to-face that evening, he probably would have stayed dead.

Ana rubbed the heel of her hand over her heart.

Why did he have to show up now? He just had to resurrect at the worst possible time.

She knew it was unfair of her to blame him for the timing, but she wanted to keep the anger simmering. It helped her focus on the task at hand.

Even as she tried to keep her mind on more pressing matters, the image of him half naked and alive within arm's reach wouldn't go away. He looked good. Really good. As handsome and perfect as she remembered him to be.

And that only pissed her off even more.

He'd obviously been doing well during his absence. So why hadn't he bothered to let her know he was alive?

The one believable conclusion was that he must have wanted her out of his life. Why else would someone go to the trouble of faking something so drastic? So then why had he sought her out tonight? Looked so happy when he'd seen her? Why did he want to talk about things so badly if there was nothing more to be said?

She jerked her mind back on track. This was exactly what she was afraid was going to happen from the moment she'd seen him. Rhys had an irritating ability to prevent her from focusing on anything or anyone else.

Not something that she would count as good, especially right now.

Shaking out her arms, she took a couple of deep breaths to center herself before reaching into her pocket and pulling out her phone. It was time for her to check in and she needed to be as calm and focused as possible to deal with the unpredictable and volatile Marco Valente.

She quickly swiped, tapped and stared at the wreckage as she waited. The painting, probably an original, had been knocked off the wall and now had a hole in it, a sculpture had been broken into shapeless shards and a decapitated lamp were going to cost a small fortune to replace.

"Ana. You have good news, I hope." The cultured, slightly accented voice masked the psycho she knew hid behind it.

Baring her teeth to the phone, she fought to keep her voice even. "Not yet, Marco. There was a slight hiccup. It won't be long before I have it, however."

"That's disappointing." His voice had gone cold. "Little Eric misses you."

Closing her eyes, Ana took a long breath. *Concentrate.* "I'll have it soon. Just make sure you keep up your end of the bargain when I do."

Rough laughter erupted over the phone. "You never cease to amuse me, Ana." He chuckled again. "I will, if you will. When have I ever reneged on a promise?"

She didn't have enough time to list them all.

It was a struggle to keep her voice steady. "I'll check in again soon."

"You do that."

Ana couldn't hang up fast enough. It was only due to her tight rein over her body and rage that she didn't throw her phone full force at the wall. That and the fact that she needed it to keep in contact with Marco.

Why had she figured that this would be a cakewalk? She had deluded herself into thinking that she was still at the top of her game. That she was invincible. Ana had wanted it to be simple because of the stakes, but the insane value of the collection being exhibited would have been enough of a lure to call out every thief and con with an ounce of skill and enough of an ego to think that they could get away with it—herself included.

But the reality of it wasn't nearly as cut and dried.

A lot could, and would, change in two years. Apparently, in the world of security technology, things had evolved by leaps and bounds. It was very serious business to constantly keep ahead of thieves. Whoever had been in charge of securing the display was good, she freely admitted that, but with a little acclimatization, Ana was confident she would come to grips with everything soon. Could she do it fast enough for Marco's liking and before someone else walked away with the prize?

Did she have any other choice?

Ana accessed the photos she had taken of the security system and of the schematics she had brought with her to compare them to the layout of the room and what she had seen that night and during the gala. What she should have done earlier was pumped Christine for more information about security. Maybe even found a guard and batted her lashes until she knew everything there was about the entire system.

But Rhys had to show up and throw her off her game.

Damn him.

What she was most irritated with was that she cared.

Ana dialed again and waited for the familiar voice to answer.

"Ana, are you on your way back?" The slight Spanish drawl was clear in his sleep-heavy voice.

It was nice that there was someone out there who was still so confident in her abilities. "There were some unexpected problems, Javier. But I should be back soon. How are things going there? How's Eric?"

"He's fine. Don't worry. I won't let anything happen to him. Marco hasn't come close to the house, though he hasn't been shy about making it known that he's watching."

Great. Wonderful.

When she didn't say anything for several moments, Javier sighed. "Is something else on your mind?"

Of course Javier would notice her agitation. They had worked together many times and were close friends. How could they not forge a tight friendship after some of the ordeals they had endured together? Over the years, they had become like brother and sister. She would have been more surprised if he hadn't said anything.

She cleared her throat. "Rhys...he's...well, here."

"What?" Alarm replaced the sleepy tone in his voice. "How is that even possible?"

"Ask yourself that for a few more hours and you might be where I am." She laughed humorlessly. "Not only that, but I'm pretty sure there's someone else after the jewel. Probably more than one, to be honest. But how is that really surprising, right?" She laughed again weakly.

She could almost imagine his frustration when he grunted the words, "Go back to that thing about Rhys. I thought he was dead."

Ana pinched the bridge of her nose. "You and me both. Apparently he's not. I found him snooping around my room earlier. When I caught him, he said he wanted to talk."

Javier let loose an aggravated snarl. "*Hijo de puta.* I'm coming up there."

"No, you're one of the few I trust to keep Eric safe. I can handle Rhys and whatever else comes my way on my own, as long as I know things are good there. I'll keep you posted on what's going on."

"Right. Be sure that you do. And, Ana?"

"Yeah?"

"Kick his ass."

That put a small smile on her face as she hung up.

Ana tossed the phone onto the rumpled bed, ignoring the flash of recollection that the tangled sheets ignited in her mind. Staying well away from it and the memories, she walked into the bathroom where she tore off her clothes and kicked them into a pile.

The night had been a total bust and left her mood and energy levels low. She might as well take a shower and think her strategy over.

The magnificence of the room wasn't lost on her. The entire hotel was a masterpiece of craftsmanship and design. And if she had a few days to spare, she would have spent some more time touring the place.

For now, she was going to take great pleasure in discovering the contents of the inside of the gleaming glass shower.

She entered it and, with a twist of her wrist, Ana turned on the water, hard and hot, then stepped under the punishing stream.

Leaning forward, she scraped her hair aside so that the full force of the water lashed her neck and upper back. It didn't take long for steam to fill the air. It whirled around her and into her lungs as she painstakingly pieced the fractured shards of her mind and concentration back together. She needed to formulate a plan that would get that gem in her hands so she could get the hell out of there as soon as possible.

The bathing products provided by the hotel were lined up according to height along the edge of the shower. The frosted swirls decorating what looked like cultivated crystals gave her the impression that they could have been snatched from the Snow Queen's own bathroom. After grabbing the closest one, Ana dumped a handful of the contents into her hand and scrubbed it into her hair.

Why did Rhys have to show up now?

Then again, would his reappearance be welcome any other time?

Once upon a time, she had prayed for what she had seen to be false. Watching the building he had been in explode then the resulting search, where recovery teams had come up with nothing, had left her with no real hope of his survival.

Then the despair had sunk in, as had the eventual

acceptance. She might not have liked it, but Ana had gotten on with her life. Even though it had been a long, slow and very painful process, she had managed it.

Then to find out he had been alive the whole time and had chosen *not* to find her or to contact her. That hurt. More than hurt. The ache in her chest returned simply from thinking about how she had mourned him, practically idolized him in her mind, when he had simply used her and moved on. And not merely in the 'sorry it's not you, it's me' kind of way. He had ripped her heart out, let her grieve, left her desolate and alone...

Ana slammed her palm against the wall, letting the stinging pain remind her just how much he had hurt her, how much damage he had done.

Then to saunter back into her life wanting to talk as if he had done nothing more than stand her up for a date? It was as infuriating as it was confusing. Did he not realize the impact of what he had done?

If Rhys thought that all it would take was a smile and a few sweet words to get in her good graces again, he was sorely mistaken.

She leaned against the wall as another series of disturbing thoughts crossed her mind.

How had he gotten into her room? He could be incredibly charming when he wanted, so had he simply convinced someone to let him in? Impossible. The staff in a hotel of this caliber would never allow it. Then there was the fact that he was staying in the penthouse. How on earth could he afford it? It was way out of the realm of possibilities for a regular consultant. It was sheer luck, and thanks to a lot of name dropping and string pulling, that she'd managed to get a room on such short notice. The penthouse at a Totally Five Star Hotel usually went to royalty or the filthy rich. So how had he pulled it off?

There were far too many questions.

Perhaps she should pin him down and get the truth out of him.

Bad choice of words.

They unleashed a torrent of scorching memories. Ones she didn't want — or need — distracting her. But there they were. Vivid and heady, as if they had occurred a moment ago. What she didn't want to admit, even to herself, was that she yearned for them to happen again. Her entire body throbbed with awareness and anticipation. As if the rest of her body didn't care what her mind wanted as long as Rhys touched her again.

Grappling with him had inadvertently given her the chance to feel his body against hers once more, though it wasn't nearly enough. He was strong, always had been, but now he seemed bigger. More intense. Even when he hadn't been trying to hurt her, Ana has felt the strength in him. The raw power.

She had yearned for more. So Ana had fought him. Had fought herself.

Which left her now more confused and angry than ever when she needed calm, concentration.

Ana let the water sluice over her, wishing that it could wash away the feelings coursing through her.

Maybe it would be for the best to hear what he had to say? It might be enough to give her closure so she could get on with her life once again. If it was good, at least she knew it wasn't all her fault for driving him away. If bad, she could peg him as a creep.

Be his reason good or utterly ridiculous, she would take it and move on.

Then she would have her precious equilibrium again.

With that plan of action in mind, Ana quickly finished washing. After getting dressed in a simple pair of jeans and T-shirt, she tied her still-wet hair into a top bun and shoved her feet into the closest pair of boots. With an oversized gray sweater thrown on top, she was ready to confront Rhys.

Chapter Three

Rhys walked down the hall, contemplating the snippets of conversation he'd heard through the frustratingly well-built door. Marco? Javier? Eric? Who were they and what were they to her?

His stomach clenched at the thought of Ana being anywhere near another man. He knew he had no right, that he had been the one to walk away, but, damn if he could be happy for her to be with someone else.

Leaving Ana had been the hardest thing he had ever had to do in his life. But it had been necessary. His beautiful, delicate Ana was too gentle and sweet. She would never survive in his world. At least that was what he used to think. He rubbed the wound on his head. If the beating she had given him earlier was any indication, she wasn't nearly as fragile as he'd thought.

He headed up to his suite, letting the thoughts run rampant in his head as he traversed the quiet halls.

She fought, not like a woman flailing to defend herself, but as someone who'd had training. And damn good training at that. Her skills were better than that of someone who had taken self-defense classes. Ana's strikes were strong, but he knew instinctively that she was pulling them. Even so, he could tell she was capable of really hurting him if she had tried. Ana might even have been able to best him if he'd let his concentration lapse.

So what did that mean?

Who was she?

Christine had introduced Ana as Countess Anastasia. Rhys had a hard time reconciling the carefree woman he'd made love to on the beach, against many walls, and many more times in a rickety, narrow bed, with the icy woman of noble rank he'd seen earlier.

Shit. He shouldn't have started thinking about Ana naked. He couldn't afford to let himself get off track. Not now. Not when he was so close.

But Ana naked… There were countless memories, many of which he revisited on long, lonely nights. Thinking of her was inevitable after seeing her again. Touching her again.

Rhys sighed. He could still smell her. Rhys could always recall her scent, even after all this time. It haunted his dreams. Now it clung to him as well as being ingrained in his mind.

What he wouldn't give for more.

The elevator opened to a long, glass-encased hall that led to the penthouse. Rhys preferred it to the ones where elevators opened up directly into the room. He knew there were safeguards, but the idea that if someone could get around the security they could also walk straight in always made him uneasy. But how different was that from any other door, really? They could all be breached with a modicum of skill and some time.

Rhys tapped his card against the reader and pushed the door open. The instant he did, all the lights came on automatically. Flinching and squinting in the glare, he cursed the individual who had come up with the idea. All he wanted was to sit and brood in the dark for the next couple of hours.

Turning off the lights from the control panel near the door, he then walked into the massive living area and straight for the fully stocked bar.

After pouring himself a couple of fingers of whiskey, he walked around, aimlessly lost in thought until he eventually found his way to the large panoramic windows that gave an unparalleled view of the surrounding area. Or at least they would if the snow let up a little.

The never-ending torrent of flakes mirrored what was

going on inside his head. His thoughts might as well have been the snow furiously whirling on the other side of the glass.

Rhys took a sip and enjoyed the way the liquid burned its way down his throat. He needed to pull his shit together, not moon over a woman who very obviously wanted nothing to do with him.

And could he blame her?

Though, at the very least, he had hoped to see some happiness in her eyes that he was alive and well. But there had been none.

Only anger. Betrayal.

He deserved it.

When he'd disappeared, he hadn't considered her feelings, had focused on his own in that he was keeping her safe. Not a thought was given to her reaction to his supposed death. He'd been so hell-bent on avenging his partner and not dragging Ana into it that he'd completely overlooked what she might have gone through.

Rhys had always planned on finding her again. Another few weeks, a couple of months at most, and he would have. He had wanted to get out of this life first. Finish one last act. Then he was all hers and he – they – would be free to be together without having to constantly be looking over his shoulder and wondering if they were truly safe. But it was never meant to go on for this long.

There was too much at stake for him to fail, so he had taken drastic action. It was meant to be temporary. He had planned to be away a week or two at the most as he hunted down the one who had killed his partner. But it had taken him two years to even get close.

Fate obviously had priority, and her plans completely shit all over his.

Fuck.

That's exactly how he felt—fucked. He'd screwed up everything with Ana and now she was all he could think about when he had other things he needed to focus on.

Rhys swirled the drink around the glass, noticing that, in the moonlight, the color almost exactly matched Ana's eyes.

The same shade they had turned when she'd looked up at him in a moonlit room, heavy-lidded and sleepy after coming apart under him. After he'd kissed and caressed her and had done his best to push her over the edge again and again before he'd followed.

He had become addicted to everything about her. Every laugh, every sigh, simply listening to her breathe as she'd slept next to him had made him want more. He needed her. Wanted her more than anything he could ever recall wanting in his life.

Rhys swallowed another mouthful of the fiery liquid, taking advantage of the distraction the burn left in its wake.

This was exactly another reason why he had chosen to stay away. Yes, he needed to keep her safe, but Ana filled his mind, his soul. He couldn't concentrate on anything else with her in his life.

He took another searing swig as there was a loud knock on his door.

Who the hell would show up this time of night?

Rhys crept toward the door. He placed the drink on the little table next to it to free up his hands in case he had to go for the gun he had hidden at his ankle. But after a quick look through the peephole, he released the breath he'd been holding.

Ana? He yanked the door open then hooked a hand around her arm to drag her in. Whatever it was had to be serious for her to show up at his door like this. "What's wrong?" She might have been dressed and her hair tugged back, but she was bedraggled and wet as though she had been caught in a storm. Her scent, however, told him otherwise. She'd been in the shower very recently and had probably been in too much of a rush to dry off. More than likely because she was worked up over something she had to say to him.

"Nothing." The way she said it through gritted teeth told him otherwise. She raked her gaze over him before flicking it over his shoulder. "Did I disturb you?"

"No. You don't look so great, though." He pushed the bounds of her compliancy a little further and pulled her farther into the suite. "Drink?"

She stared at him, long and hard, as if she was still trying to believe that he was really standing in front of her.

"Ana?"

She focused her eyes on his. "Is Christine here?"

Her voice was so low he wasn't sure that he'd heard her. "Christine? No. Why would she be?"

His reply only succeeded in having her sweep the immediate area with her gaze. "You were her date. I figured you two were together."

He shook his head. "It's not like that."

Because he figured she needed it, he pressed his drink into her hand. "Drink."

Amazingly, she did. She spluttered and coughed, but she took another sip before pushing it back into his grasp.

"I came here for answers." She looked him directly in the eyes. "I need to know why you did what you did so I can get on with my life. Again."

So she expected to just walk out of his life when they'd scarcely been reunited? The thought curdled into a ball of dread at the pit of his gut. There had to be something he could do to defuse the situation.

He ushered her to the couch and waited until she robotically sat on one end then he took the other. Rhys desperately wanted to get closer to her, touch her, but she looked as though she needed space. He was willing to give it to her. At least for now.

She studied him again, leaving him feeling as though she had stabbed him with her eyes. "When I left my room, I was pretty sure I wanted to kick your ass. Then somewhere in between there and your door…the urge completely died."

Rhys didn't need her to explain. He could see it clearly

on her face. She was defeated. Tired. It twisted something inside him, seeing her so void and knowing it was his fault.

Clenching his fists, he tried to catch her gaze. "I always meant to come find you, Ana. You have to know that."

Fire blazed in her eyes. "Did you? Faking your own death seems pretty permanent."

The bile with which she said the words flayed him. "It was to keep you safe." It was half-true, at least.

That caught her attention. She zeroed in on his eyes and held his gaze with unnerving scrutiny. "From what?"

"I can't tell you."

When she would have gotten up, Rhys gripped her wrist and gently held her back. "This is why I did what I did. It kills me to keep things from you, but you have to understand they're for your own good."

She glared daggers at him. "I think I know what's for my own good."

Anger licked at his gut. Annoyance crackled between them.

"This is what I'm talking about," he groused.

"What? That I want to know what's so huge that you had to, in essence, kill yourself to get away from me?"

Rhys was the one to get up. He slammed the drink onto the coffee table and stalked the ample space on the other side. "That I want to tell you everything. That I don't want there to be any secrets between us. That you will keep digging until you get what you want because I'm too weak to deny you and it will get you hurt."

"Because you…want to protect me from some mysterious danger that will certainly spell my doom…" Ana mocked him with a sneer, plainly intent on making it a fight.

He wasn't going to let her and continued, genuinely, steadily holding her gaze. "I would do anything if it meant keeping you safe."

"But you're so sure that this secret of yours will hurt me that you've been willing to let me think you were dead for two years." She let out a growl. "You know what hurt me?

Thinking you were dead! If anyone hurt me, it was you!"

Rhys dragged his hands through his hair as he glared down at her. "It wasn't supposed to go on for this long. I was coming to get you as soon as it was over."

"Right." She shot to her feet. "I guess this was a total waste of time. Why did you even suggest... You know what?" Ana flung her hands up, as if she was throwing away any notion of trying to sort things out between them. "If you're not willing to tell me anything, I might as well leave."

She stalked past him, but instinct had Rhys grabbing her hand and keeping her from fleeing from his life.

"Ana, it's almost done. I would have gone to find you within a few weeks. Probably right after New Year."

"That's convenient, isn't it?" She wrenched her hand from his grasp. "Don't bother trying to find me once whatever it is you're doing is over, because I won't be waiting for you."

The echo of her boots on the wooden floor punctuated her anger as she stomped toward the door.

He watched her, knowing that if she walked out now there was a good chance he'd never get the chance to speak to her again. Rhys didn't go after her but couldn't stop the whispered words, "What we had was good, Ana."

His soft entreaty stopped her dead in her tracks. Whirling on her heel, she glared at him before rushing back toward him.

She stopped close enough to jab a finger in his chest. "It was. At least I thought it was. I used to think about our time together fondly." There was an all too brief wistful expression on her face that burned away in the wake of her anger. "Not anymore. You destroyed it with what you did. How can I possibly believe that any of it was real? That anything that comes out of your mouth now is true?"

He knew what they had was still there. At least for him. Ana might be pissed off, but she couldn't pretend that there was nothing still simmering between them. That what had once burned so hot and bright was lost. He knew she still cared. It had been etched on her face in the moments when she'd first seen him again. Before she'd shut herself off to him.

A reminder was in order.

Rhys snared her hand again, but this time, he reeled her in until he'd wrapped himself around her. If he needed to prompt her of the passion that he remembered so well, then so be it.

Giving into the need to taste Ana again, Rhys crashed his mouth down on hers.

She fought him. Clawed his arms. Tried to tear them away. Incrementally, the shoves and protests weakened. The twists to get away morphed into writhing as she rubbed herself against him. The angry cries became moans of frustration when he had to tear his mouth from hers for air. Ana clutched him tightly to her, as if she couldn't get close enough—like she would never let go—then dragged him down for another searing kiss.

His body's reaction to her was immediate and Rhys was more than willing to let Ana in on the fact, as well. Cupping her ass, he made sure there was no question about whether or not he felt the heat smoldering between them. From the way she ground herself along his cock, Ana was as caught up as he was, and she wasn't complaining.

Rhys changed the angle of the kiss, didn't give a damn that his lungs burned. That his head swam. Not when her tongue met his at first with a shy brush that then turned into a sure stroke. The taste of her intoxicated him. As did her scent. The years fell away until, once more, they were simply a couple deeply in love, enjoying a private moment together. From thighs, to hips, to chest, every inch of Ana's lush body was pressed up flush to him and her impatient writhing rucked up her sweater, inviting his hands to explore her silky, soft skin.

Sliding them under, Rhys reveled in the sensation of her, warm and vibrant under his palms. He gently skimmed the flat of her stomach, up over her ribs. His explorations farther upward found, to his delight, that she wore no bra.

She filled his hands perfectly, just as he remembered. Rhys couldn't help but cup and weigh the perfect globes, squeezing gently. Ana arched into his hands, wanting more of his touch.

Rhys pushed the fabric up out of his way so he could close his lips around a greedy peak. She bowed her back and thrust herself farther into his mouth. Rhys sucked and flicked his tongue over the hard tip and relished the way she trembled in reaction. With a groan, he circled it before moving to her other breast.

Sliding her hands into his hair, Ana held him close. Pulling him closer. She clawed him lustfully as he grazed her nipple with his teeth.

It was her groaned name, rough and unbidden from his lips that seemed to snap Ana out of it.

Breathing as heavily as Rhys, Ana glared at him, eyes flashing angrily as she wrenched her clothing back in place. She took an unsteady pace back, then another. "You will never do that again." Her tone might have been hard, but the breathlessness of her voice gave her away.

He'd probably lose an arm or an eye in the process the next time he risked kissing her, but it would happen and it would absolutely be worth it.

Later.

Right now, that one spectacular kiss had to hold him over.

Rhys simply smiled, walked over to the door and held it open for her. This time, there was no doubt in his mind that he would be seeing her — and kissing her — again soon.

"See you around."

"Not if I can help it," she groused.

He only smiled at the way her words sounded smoky and sleepy.

Yeah, he would.

Chapter Four

Ana stalked down the hall, half-furious and half-dazed, entirely turned on and frustrated. How dare he kiss her? How dare he put his hands all over her as if he had the right to?

How dare it feel so damned good?

She would never admit it to him, but the kiss, the feel of his skin against hers was amazing. Incredible. So missed. And curse her for wanting more. Her entire body hummed, aching for more of his touch.

Rhys looked too good. Felt too good. Tasted too good. It was as if he had engineered it all that way solely to drive her crazy. Handsome as ever, the solitary thing about him that seemed a little different than she remembered was the look in his eyes. There was something new there. Darker, serious, a little sad. Ana instinctively wanted to do whatever it took to erase it. Another thing that pissed her off.

What was he hiding? What was so dangerous that he felt had to fake his own death? Ana had a hard time believing that someone as sweet and gentle as Rhys could be involved in anything that would hurt her.

The idea of it was absurd. Yet he seemed so utterly convinced he had done the right thing that he radiated with conviction.

Either he believed it or he had become a very good liar.

But hadn't that ruse with Christine proved that he was adept, at the very least? Then there was the unwillingness to talk, even when he was the one who had the gall to tell her to come find him when she was ready for some answers.

He had extended an olive branch only for it to be a

complete lie. Had Rhys said it merely to get her to come to his suite? To kiss her?

It had been hell of a lot more than a simple kiss. Ana licked her lips again thinking about it. She could still taste him and that served to confuse her more and fuel the throbbing ache inside her.

It left her head reeling and her gut filled with burning anger.

Or was it arousal?

How strange was it that the sensations felt so much alike?

Ana hated that Rhys had gotten to her so easily. That one kiss was all it had taken to shake apart the walls she had erected against him. Ana knew that letting him touch her would mess with her head. Then to kiss him? It was stupid and reckless...and so good. As delicious as it was, she wasn't going to let it happen again. Not if she was going to keep her head in gear.

There was the niggling question of what he thought he was protecting her from, however. If it was even true. And if it was, everything about his involvement in something that dangerous should have been reason enough for her to walk away. Whatever it was, was something big enough to derail her life over, so she was going to find out what it was.

But finding out about Rhys' past was secondary to everything else. It had waited this long, a little while more wouldn't make much of a difference.

What could optimistically be called daylight dimly lit the halls from the large windows on the ends of the corridor, but even before she reached them, Ana knew that she wasn't going to like what she saw outside.

The edge of the window gathered a thick layer of snow that obscured most of the glass. What she could see on the other side was nothing but more snow. It didn't bode well for a departure tonight.

Continuing on toward her suite, Ana pieced together what she knew about the exhibition in order to rethink her plans. A storm could be a good thing. It would give her time to work out the kinks and figure out an exit strategy. On the downside, said exit would have to be timed to perfection and a deluge of snow wasn't going to facilitate that.

As she walked past an older couple, presumably out for an early morning stroll, she smiled. Well dressed and totally suited to the luxuriant atmosphere of the hotel, they made an adorable pair. Ana once imagined what she and Rhys would be like in the future. It was a fleeting thought, but it had led her to envisage them to be like the twosome tottering past. Close. Happy. Obviously still so very much in love.

Sighing, she doggedly kept up her pace as she overheard their quiet conversation debating the merits of being trapped in the hotel for the foreseeable future.

Ana couldn't help the shiver skittering down her spine at the thought. The longer she was stuck there, the worse things would get. Marco wasn't a patient man. Or a very predictable one. He was deadly and ruthless, which kept her in a constant state of paranoia, wondering if each text or call would be the one letting her know he had snapped.

Then there was being trapped in a hotel with Rhys, which most definitely wasn't going to help matters. Especially when he seemed particularly determined to revive their past relationship.

So much to deal with… It was threatening to make her head spin.

By the time she arrived at her suite, Ana had to forcibly control her breathing. Slowly. In and out through her clenched teeth as she tried to calm the thundering of her heart. Losing it wasn't going to help her. Inside the collection of rooms assigned to her once more, Ana's lungs cooperated a bit more, but the suite she once thought of as her haven had been ruined by Rhys' intrusion.

Now the walls were a cage that seemed to be closing in on her.

She headed to the window in the hopes that the view would help calm her a little but, like before, Ana could see nothing but white. The sky, the air filled with flakes, the ground, were all a monotonous white adding to the sensation of being closed in. So much for that idea.

Ana figured it wouldn't be too early to call Javier and check on how things were going on his end. At the very least she could keep him apprised of the situation there.

She dialed and was almost immediately rewarded with his voice. "Ana? What's the matter?"

"Snowstorm. I might be stuck here a while. How are things there?"

"Nothing has changed here, though when Marco hears that you're going to be delayed, he might not be too happy."

Ana sighed. "Which is why I wanted you to know first. You need to make sure Eric stays safe." Marco was desperate and unhinged enough to do something neither of them could anticipate.

"We could use some help. I'm good, but I can't protect Eric and defend against Marco at the same time. Especially if he goes on the rampage."

Ana quickly ran through a mental list of trusted friends in the area. "Can you get in touch with Sara? We can trust her."

"I'll call, though it would probably be better if you do it. The last time we were on a job together we were stuck in a cellar for days." There was a short pause full of things unsaid as he sighed. "Let's just say, the experience hardly endeared us to each other."

She ran her hand over her face. She'd forgotten about Javier and Sara being trapped together. They had gone in as flirty friends and come out the other end never wanting to speak to each another again. Ana never did get the story behind it, but she could guess.

"Sara being there won't be a problem, will it?"

"It won't be. Don't worry. There's much more at stake here than... Eric's more important." Another longer pause followed. "Have you talked to Rhys at all?"

"I did talk to Rhys." Ana's mind immediately flashed a

reminder that talking wasn't the only thing they'd done. Her breasts ached in response. "But it was completely pointless."

"Why am I not surprised?"

"You can do something else for me, too. Think you're up to performing a quick background check?"

Javier chuckled. "You could challenge me a bit more."

"Well look up Rhys and — or — Richard Stone."

A scoff came from Javier. "He's having an identity crisis?"

Ana snorted. "I'm having a little trouble believing he's who he says he is right now."

"Sounds intriguing."

"Intriguing, my ass. Try horrible. He's a liar and that pisses me off." And confused the hell out of her.

Javier sighed. "I can understand how betrayed you feel —"

"Can you? I doubt it," she grumped into the phone.

Javier continued, as if she hadn't said a thing, "But maybe he had a good reason."

Ana gripped the phone tighter, as if doing so would help her throttle the man on the other end. Or maybe even the one with her in the hotel. "What is it with guys thinking they can do whatever they like if they think it's in your best interest? Don't we get a say in the matter? It's not like we don't have brains in our heads. How would we ever survive without a big, strong man protecting us from the world?"

"Okay... I think we just went to a bad place." Javier groaned, sounding like he was sitting up. "I'm only saying he might have thought he was sparing you from something and that shouldn't be discounted."

And she wasn't ignoring that. What irked her was that he didn't trust her enough to tell her what was going on and give her the choice in the matter.

"Thanks so much for your input." Ana didn't even try to put any love in her words.

Javier sighed. "Like you ever take any notice."

"Remember that time in Oaxaca? I listened to you then and you've never let me forget it."

"You paid attention to my idea because you didn't have a choice," he grumbled. "So the plan is that I'll call Sara and see if she'll come and help, then I'll look into your miraculously resurrected boyfriend. Anyone or anything else I should do?"

So many things. But Ana kept it short and simple. "Do whatever you think you need to do to keep Eric safe. How much time do you want before I call Marco?"

He took a moment to think about it. "Give me thirty minutes. That'll be enough time to get set up here. Just in case."

"Thanks, Javier." She was blessed to have someone in her life that she could trust so absolutely.

"You owe me three now."

Ana chuckled. "Just tell me how and when I can repay you and it's done."

She swiped the phone, ending the call and tapped her forehead with it a few times. With one last smack, she slipped it into her pocket.

Thirty minutes would give her time to try to line things up, at least as much as she was able, before talking to Marco.

There was entirely too much up in the air and planning was going to be a nightmare with the goal line constantly moving. She needed more information about the exhibits. Flaws. Exploits she could employ. Details about the security. The movements of the guards. Then Ana needed a little cooperation from Mother Nature, which would a bit harder to get.

One thing at a time.

Ana quickly replaced her relaxed clothing with something more suited to the hotel's ambience. It was time for some recon.

The plain and comfortable was replaced by chic dove-gray, wide-legged trousers and a burgundy sweater with a plunging neckline. Her hair was left to fall in a curtain of waves over her shoulders and down her back. With strategically added glitter, Ana looked as any other woman who spent all her life in hotels like this.

Hopefully she'd be able to get some details out of a security guard who would be easily sidetracked with a smile and some cleavage.

She applied a touch of makeup and shrugged. It was the best she was going to manage at the moment. The sleepless night had dulled her skin and dimmed her eyes. Or it could have been all thanks to the confrontation with Rhys.

Not that she wanted to rehash that.

Regardless, no amount of makeup was going to help.

Ana leisurely made her way down to one of the restaurants, knowing that whichever one she picked would be wonderful. Because she was in the mood to stare into the blank whiteness that was outside, she chose the one with the biggest windows, at least according to the brochures.

The restaurant was supposed to make a diner feel as if they were eating on the edge of the world, only now, it was more like the world had been enveloped in a fluffy, white goose down. Blank and clean. Perfect to stare at as she contemplated her situation.

She imagined what it would look like on a bright, sunny day. The sun would illuminate the beautiful mountainside and the area below. The sky would be brilliant blue and the rock would be broken up with flowers and some greenery before it dropped out from below and spread out into a vibrantly valley.

Inside was equally as beautiful.

The various woods that decorated and made up the furnishings were wonderfully grained and could almost be paint strokes. Subtle yet enough to catch the eye and invite a study of the craftsmanship.

Ana gazed out of the window. She found the stark whiteness quite spectacular in its own right. There was beauty in the unsoiled white on white. It gave her the impression that the world beyond these walls was fresh. Pristine. Though she knew it was far from it. She had learned some harsh truths about humanity growing up, becoming who she was now. The things she had seen over the years had taught her that people, while they could be wonderful, were also the cause of some of her worst memories.

Greed, lust for power — for sex — and the many lies she'd heard and had told weighed on her mind. It didn't come easily to her. Learning to do it convincingly had been arduous. Even after all this time, she still preferred to skirt the truth rather than flat out lie.

This time, however, there was little guilt. She was willing to do whatever it took to see it through. As the last job she would ever take, Ana was only there this time because she had been coerced. Once it was over she intended to live out the rest of her life in anonymity and seclusion.

Rhys didn't enter the equation at any point of her plans.

By the time the maître d' led her to a table next to the window, her mood had plummeted. Not staring at the flakes as they danced and whirled outside, studying the menu and architecture or trying to plan out her next move managed to derail her morose train of thought.

It wasn't long before a handsome waiter appeared at her side.

"*Bon matin*. I'm Gregoire, your waiter this morning." He smiled cheerfully and carefully kept his gaze from wandering too low, though she knew the golden chains dangling in the daring V drew his attention and sorely tempted him to look.

"Good morning, Gregoire." Ana gave the menu a cursory glance. "Strong black coffee and a croissant, please."

"At once." He rushed away just as a figure dressed in a dark suit approached her table.

"A beautiful woman such as you shouldn't be eating alone."

Ana lifted her gaze to meet the smiling face of Diego Cabral. "Mr. Cabral."

"Such formality, my dear countess. I thought we became better friends than that last night."

She somehow managed to muster a wan smile. The last

thing she needed was to have to fend off his advances while she tried to get her head together. "But you broke my heart last night, disappearing as you did."

He slid his hand over the back of the chair. "I'm here now to make up for that."

Ana pouted, hoping he would take the hint. "I was enjoying a moment to myself, actually."

"Well, now we can enjoy a moment together." He pulled out the seat and was about to sit when another figure approached.

"I'm sorry, darling. I was held up with a call." Rhys gave her a proprietary peck on the cheek before turning to smile at the other man. "Morning."

Ana wasn't sure if she was happy or not to see Rhys insinuate himself between Cabral and the table. He stood in front of the empty seat as if he didn't appreciate the other man infringing on his territory.

"Who's this?" Cabral eyed Rhys from head to toe and back up again, sneering at him as if Rhys was dirt on his shoe.

"Richard Stone." Rhys held out his hand, a charmingly relaxed smile on his face. "An old…*friend* of the countess."

Biting her tongue, Ana barely managed to keep herself from kicking Rhys in the shin for the way he'd said friend. As far as male posturing went, he'd made it very clear to the other man that she had been claimed by him. And he was willing to take him on if he pushed the matter. She took Rhys' hand and dug her nails into his palm. It simply made him smile more.

Luckily, the ruse worked. Perhaps he didn't want to make a scene or he was bowing out when faced with a more powerful man, but the hopeful expression that had been on Cabral's face dimmed. "I see."

Rhys settled into the seat with the air of a king claiming his throne. "You're welcome to join us, of course."

"I wouldn't want to intrude." Cabral caught Ana's gaze once more. "I hope to see you around, Countess."

And with that, he walked straight out of the restaurant.

Rhys chuckled. "I guess I ruined his appetite."

Cabral wasn't the only one to have lost interest in eating.

Ana glared at him as he casually waved a waiter over. "What do you think you're doing?"

Her unwelcome dining companion shrugged. "Saving you from that creep. I have to say, I'm not impressed by the friends you've been making." Rhys eyed her critically as he made himself comfortable.

Ana bristled. "You have no say on the company I keep. I was dealing with him fine on my own. And you're not staying, so don't bother ordering."

Completely unfazed, he smirked. "You've really gotten bossy, you know that?"

"How would you know? Our entire time together was spent…" Heat blasted her cheeks when she remembered exactly how they had spent their time together in the past.

"Well, I don't remember you making many demands back then. Except maybe 'harder' or 'deeper'." He leaned in closer. "And my personal favorite, 'Make me scream, Rhys' which was always my pleasure to facilitate."

Gregoire, of course, chose that moment to appear and to carefully place her coffee and croissant on the table in front of her before making a tactfully hasty retreat.

With her face burning up, she glared at Rhys. Christ. Didn't the man know when to keep his mouth shut? His words, however, caused her mind to flash back to those particular occasions, leaving her mouth dry and her hands trembling.

She had to get out of there. Away from him. "If you're not leaving, I will." She shoved her seat back and stood.

Rhys simply watched her with an amused glint in his eyes. "We're going to be stuck in this place for the next few days at least, so you're going to have to get used to the idea of running into me."

She flipped her hair over her shoulder. "There's a huge difference between running into you as we pass in the halls and you barging in uninvited on my breakfast."

Rhys put up his hands. "I'm sorry I ruined your breakfast with the charming Mr. Cabral. I didn't know it was that important to you."

Ana was milliseconds from making a scene and dug her nails into her palms to keep from doing so. "What I take offense at is that you seem to think that you have some place in my life."

He reached over and tried to take hold of her hand but sighed when she jerked it out of reach. "Will you just sit down so we can have breakfast?"

"Have mine."

Rhys narrowed his dark eyes as he gazed at her scornfully. "I never took you for a coward."

"How dare you." Ana clamped down on the anger as best she could. He was goading her and she wasn't going to fall for it. "If anyone here is a coward, it's you."

Leaning back in his chair, he crossed his arms, making the hard lines of them clear even through the sweater he wore. "I'm not the one who's running."

"And I'm not the one who's hiding things."

His jaw dropped before he let loose a bark of laughter. "Let's talk about hiding things, shall we? What's a *countess* doing with a grappling hook in her bag?"

So he *had* searched through her things. The bastard. She ignored the voice in her head calling her a hypocrite when she formulated the easy lie. "I'm a climber. I had hoped to do some while I'm here." It was true, to a point.

"So where's the rest of your equipment? All I saw was one pitiful rope in your bag."

Ana gritted her teeth and forced her breath through them. "Like I said, I had *hoped* to climb. They were lost in transit."

"Such a shame. I bet the storm is making it hard, too. You used to love the outdoors. Do you still?"

Knowing he was alluding to how they'd spent their time together outdoors, she wasn't going to answer him. Turning the questioning around, Ana stared down her nose at him. "Why do you care? And if we're talking about cowards, let's talk about you. What are you hiding from me, *Richard*?"

His expression shuttered at the use of his alias.

"Exactly, it's fine for me to spill my guts to you, but when I ask for a little reciprocation you refuse. So who's the coward now?"

Rhys stood and rounded the table to loom over her.

When she would have backed away, he held her fast, gripping her hand tightly with his much larger ones.

Rhys peered deep into her eyes, as if he wanted her to see every emotion he was feeling. "Yes, I refuse to answer and I'm going to continue to do so because it'll keep you safe. That might make me a coward, but only because I was—I am—afraid of losing you. So, yeah, feel free to hate the selfish prick who lied because he doesn't want to think of a world that doesn't have you in it. Call me all the names you want as long as you have the breath to do so. It'll be worth it if it keeps you alive."

Ana stared at him. How could she believe a word out of his mouth?

The thing was, she did. The depth of feeling in his words, the passion in his eyes. Rhys believed every word of what he was saying.

It only made her curiosity that much stronger.

Who was Rhys Stone and what secrets did he hide?

Ana pushed her seat back and strode out of the room.

Chapter Five

Without the teeming crowds, Ana had to work harder at not being conspicuous when, once again, she found herself wandering through the exhibit. According to the guard she had spoken to earlier, the security for the room was top notch. It had been created from the ground up to suit the very specific needs that a display such as this one had. He'd been so proud of the fact, that anyone listening to him would think that he'd been the one to design it.

She'd poked and prodded and needled for more information as she'd listened with feigned wide-eyed wonder. But what he'd given her had had Ana cursing her luck. Being out of the game for so long would make it hard to handle a job like this on a truncated timetable. Anyone who knew anything about the world she had tried so hard to leave behind would know that two years might as well have been millennia. Even when she'd been at the top of her game, it would have taken weeks of planning and a team of specialists to pull off something like this.

Her latest call to Javier hadn't done anything to boost her confidence. Marco was getting antsy. He'd even started approaching the house, making it abundantly clear that he could, and would, attack if he felt slighted.

Wanting to judge for herself, Ana dialed Marco. She willed her hand to stop trembling as she waited through the ring tone.

"Ana, I hope you have some good news for me."

He sounded calm. Perhaps more than he should be. "I'm only keeping you in the loop like you wanted, Marco."

"That's a shame. I'm so looking forward to my new

bauble. I know Eric would love to play with it."

"You know the deal. I get it for you, and you're out of our lives."

"Just as soon as you bring it to me." His mild tone raised her hackles even further. "Because as you said, we have a deal."

"I'll get it to you soon. The storm is making it impossible for me to gauge timescales."

Ana waited for what felt like an eternity for his reply.

"I've always thought that mothers would do absolutely anything for their children. I guess that's another lie." Ana took a breath to retort, but he continued. "Maybe you need more incentive. Snow is nothing, isn't it? Merely frozen water. What's that thing people say about blood? That it's thicker than water? Do they specify if it's animal blood or human? Adult's or a child's?"

"Marco—"

He voice was controlled, cold, as he spoke, "If you don't bring that diamond to me soon, I'm just going to have to find out. I don't care if there is snow. I don't care if it's the Apocalypse. I *want* that diamond. You think that your one pathetic guard is going to stop me from getting to your son?"

Ana fought to keep her voice steady. "I'll get it. You have my word. Have a little patience."

"No. You need to figure out how to get it to me soon, or your precious boy *will* have an accident."

Ana closed her eyes and shoved the phone in her pocket. Obviously thinking that he would be patient because of a storm was too much to hope for.

Stifling the fear, she gathered her wits and went to stare at the diamond for the third time that day.

It didn't help that the faceoff with Rhys that morning still haunted her and muddled her concentration more.

Javier's search for Rhys hadn't found anything about him which was statistically impossible. Everyone left a trail that someone like Javier could uncover. No matter how random or insignificant, there was always something to dig up. That lack of information meant he didn't exist or he hid his identity incredibly well.

Either way, Rhys was no regular consultant.

There were many possibilities. Too many to count, especially with her imagination and experience. She'd dealt with her fair share of liars and cheats and scum. Up to the point she'd met Rhys, she'd thought all men were the same. Until recently, she'd believed him to be the exception.

How ironic that she'd been right all along.

At least about the lying part.

The reason for that lie, however, was up for debate.

Could Rhys truly believe that he was protecting her? A small part of her acknowledged the idea was romantic. Extremely so. But that was only if what he said was true. That was what she was hung up on.

What could he believe to be so dangerous that he had to pretend to be dead in order to secure her safety?

That question was one of the thoughts keeping her preoccupied all day when she should have been focused on getting the jewel and getting the hell out of there.

What bothered her the most was the relentless ache that had plagued her since seeing Rhys again. Ana couldn't forget the feel of his hands on her. The taste of his mouth, the texture of it against hers again. She still wanted him, wanted more of what he could do to her—there was no denying that—but there was more than sating her lust that mattered here.

It didn't stop her from reliving the kiss over and over again in the midst of replaying some of their hotter encounters in her mind. It was as though their earlier kiss had unlocked the floodgates and she was helpless to stop the torrent of memories that now saturated her brain with hormones. It made it incredibly difficult to think, let alone come up with a plan that wouldn't land her in prison, or worse.

Still, her breasts ached, wanting more of his touch. Even in a room with people milling about, Ana bit her lip to keep from moaning his name at the memories. Her skin was hot and sensitive. The throbbing at the apex of her thighs wouldn't abate. And she knew she would continue to be distracted and irritatingly achy until she got naked with him.

Just as she had back in Positano.

There was no other time in her life that she'd let loose and felt so relaxed and carefree. Rhys had played a huge part in that.

Who was she kidding? He had been the reason she had been so happy and relaxed.

Boneless might have been a better way of describing her state back then. They had given and taken pleasure in equal measures and were left sated and replete as a result for most of their time together. Rhys had made sure that there wasn't a part of her that went unexplored, and that went for kinks she never knew she had.

Licking her lips, Ana recalled just how often they'd found themselves hot and bothered in places where they could easily have gotten caught, once he'd realized how much it turned her on. Or how restraining him had been empowering for her.

And vice versa.

Ana tingled from head to toe as the images flashed through her mind.

There wasn't a thing they'd been unwilling to try. There had been no judgement, no censure. Only pleasure. Even when they hadn't been naked, they had talked for hours, had connected on more than a physical basis until she had been sure she had found *the* one. It had all been so perfect.

But, apart from the stellar sex, how much of everything else they had shared was real?

Ana dislodged the thoughts from her mind with a shake of her head. She couldn't afford to waste her time thinking about Rhys.

She stared at the podium and pictured the tech and wiring inside. What they connected to. Ways to circumvent them…

"You must really like diamonds."

Speak of the devil.

She didn't bother turning to look at him. "Name a woman who doesn't."

Rhys took the spot to her right and crossed his arms as he stared at the glass-encased gem. "I don't know what's so special about them. It's a sparkly rock."

"To some, maybe. It's so much more to me." She angled her head slightly so she could see his expression. "Or I have nothing better to do since we're trapped in this hotel."

Ana caught the roll of his eyes.

"If you were bored you could have said something."

She shook her head. "I'm quite happy doing this, thanks."

Rhys wound a warm arm around her waist. "Come on. We're probably going to be here for a few days more, they'll still be here. Tomorrow."

Would they? Ana wasn't so sure.

As much as she wanted to stand and stare until a plan miraculously popped into her head, Ana didn't want to draw attention to herself. At least no more than she already had by continually showing up to ogle. There was only so much she could play off as just being a diamond-obsessed countess with too much time on her hands.

Maybe a break *was* in order.

So she let him lead her out of the room. Ana didn't want to like the feel of his arm around her, but she did. Too much. It brought back memories of when they used to go on long walks together on the rocky cliffs of the Italian coast.

When they'd first met and walked from the restaurant to her flat, he had wound himself around her in the same way. And for every walk they'd gone on afterward.

Ana allowed a small smile to curve her lips at the recollection of their meeting. It was a well-trod memory, both romantic and sensual.

The job she had been doing in the small coastal village had gone well. It had been a simple matter of retrieving a painting that had been stolen months before from a museum that had reappeared in the home of a less than scrupulous aristocrat. The man needed to spend more on security and less on art that didn't belong to him. A week of recon and a little planning and the job had gone without a hitch.

Just as she'd been about to pack up and leave, Ana had decided to have one last meal at a restaurant that had become a favorite of hers during her stay. She'd been minding her own business, enjoying the view of the ocean from the balcony, when she'd looked across the room and her gaze had collided with Rhys'. His hair had been a bit longer and wilder. He was tanned from the sultry sun and he'd been dressed casually in a linen shirt that he'd left the top buttons undone on, giving her a glimpse of more skin. His smile had been small, almost shy at first, but had slowly widened with each glance. And each time she'd taken more of him in. The breadth of his shoulders had filled out the shirt nicely, the tanned forearms bare and toned. His legs, long and lean, encased in dark trousers stretched out under his table.

Ana wasn't ashamed to admit that, on her part, it had been lust at first sight. The rest of the meal had been spent meeting glances and sharing little smiles until he'd finally come to join her. His offering of the most heavenly tiramisu had broken the ice and they'd sat and talked until she and Rhys closed out the restaurant.

Rhys had claimed to be a tech consultant of some sort who was in from England and had decided to take a long-needed break in Positano on his way back up to Rome before flying back.

Totally out of character for her, Ana had blamed it on the romance of the night, the atmosphere, even the food as the reasons that she had taken him straight back to the tiny apartment she had been renting. There they had stayed for the majority of the next few breathless months.

She'd wanted to believe that the whole affair had been fate finally giving her something good. After all the shit and horribleness that had been her experience with men up until then, she'd been gifted with her other half. Their relationship had been so romantic and wonderful. It had been so easy. Everything had simply seemed to fall into place, and Ana had been felt as though she had truly found the part of herself that had been missing.

The idyllic, dreamlike state she had found herself in had been shattered when he had to be the hero and run into a burning building to save some children who they had come to recognize on their walks. He had managed to come out with three and left them with her to go searching for their missing puppy.

Ana had never felt such clawing terror as she had watching him go back in. Or such numbing shock when, as she'd prepared to go in after him, the building had exploded into the night.

She had grieved for him ever since.

And it had all been a lie.

The hole in her heart that she wanted to believe had healed had split open once again.

Rhys jostled her gently. "You're quiet."

She shrugged, easing a little space between them. "Only reevaluating the past couple of years."

Rhys took a moment to digest that before he spoke again, quietly asking, "Where did you go after Positano?"

She'd traveled the world, losing herself in work for a few months until she settled in a secluded mill house in the south of France. Far from everything that she had been in the past. In the end, it had all been futile. Her old life had found her.

"Here and there."

He took that with a stoic silence. Rhys had to know that opening up to him again was going to be hard for her after everything.

"I returned to England for a while."

Ana turned her stunned gazed to him. Was he actually talking about himself? In spite of the shock, she was interested in what he had to share and listened intently.

"I was so churned up about what had happened — what I did — that I didn't stay long. I threw myself into work, wanting only to get that part of my life over with so I could return to you again."

Her smile was small. "And what line of work would that be again?"

She caught the upward twitch of his lips.

"Consulting."

"For?"

He squeezed her teasingly. "Let's stick with consulting for now."

The tension that had shrouded her since seeing him again was slowly starting to lift. If she was being truthful, it had started dissipating with his confession at breakfast. It was starting to feel like old times.

Something she couldn't afford right now.

Ana stepped out of his grasp. The less he touched her, the better. It seemed that everything about him, from the feel of him against her skin to his scent to just seeing his smile, scrambled her brains.

Keeping her distance, she asked, "Where are we going?"

"They have an amazing lounge. It's usually used for relaxing *après* ski, but since there isn't much chance of getting out on the slopes…"

He slowed and turned to take in her reaction to the room.

Ana was awestruck by the breadth and beauty of the room. It was spectacular as was expected of a Totally Five Star Hotel. It had the warm, cozy feeling of a ski lodge but multiplied by many times. The massive panes of glass piled on top of one another until they reached a peak to give a view of the majestic mountains outside. Or it would have if there wasn't so much snow veiling them.

Rustic wooden chandeliers dangled from the ceiling to illuminate the room with warm pools of light. Huge couches and chairs were strategically placed to facilitate conversation and enjoyment of the view. But what caught her attention was the massive circular fireplace that served as the center point of the room. It was perfect for relaxing after a ski…or for a romantic interlude.

Neither of which she was doing right now.

"It's beautiful." She turned on her heel and started back the way they'd come.

He caught up with her in a few short strides. "Then where are you going?"

"Away from here." And far away from him.

He circled around her to step into her path. "What's wrong?"

"I don't know what you think you're doing, but I'm not having any part of it." She couldn't. There was too much to deal with right now to allow herself to lose focus.

He didn't budge. "This place is made for relaxation. Why not take advantage of it while we can?"

"I don't have that luxury." Ana skirted around him and started walking as fast as she could without breaking into a sprint.

He grasped her hand. "Then why are you here? Why come to a luxury hotel, where relaxation and indulgence is an implied part of the itinerary, if that's not what you're going to do?"

She wrenched her hands from his. So he'd brought her there to try to worm information out of her. Why was she surprised? "I don't have to explain myself to you."

"You're right, you don't. I was only hoping that we could talk and reconnect." He put up his hands and stepped back. "It's clear you want to do neither. Do whatever you have to do."

"Countess? Richard?" Christine walked hurriedly down the hall toward them with a grin on her face. "I was hoping I'd run into at least one of you. I'm going crazy wandering around this place on my own."

Ana gave her a tight smile. "Perfect." It dimmed a little when she looked at Rhys. "*Richard* here was just saying the same thing. You two can keep each other company while I retire to my room. I've got a bit of a headache, but at least now I can rest easy knowing I won't be leaving him all alone. Goodnight."

She stalked down the hall and almost immediately regretted it when she was spotted by Ciara.

"Anastasia! Can you believe the weather? Although being trapped here isn't exactly a hardship, is it? Have you seen Esteban?"

The hotel was huge, sprawling, in fact. So why did it feel as if they were all crammed in a shoebox together? Ana decided to focus on the last question since it was probably the single one Ciara cared about anyway.

She shook her head. "I haven't seen Esteban around."

Ciara heaved a sigh. "Oh, well, he's bound to turn up. Feel like a drink?"

"I was actually heading back to my suite to nurse a headache."

Ciara pouted. "You poor dear. Are you sure it isn't something a little company can cure?"

She must have been really desperate for companionship. Or gossip. Unfortunately for her, Ana wasn't in the mood to try to play along. "I think it would be better for me to have a nice warm bath and an early night."

Ciara's pout turned into a frown. "Well, you know your body best. Maybe we can have lunch tomorrow if we're still stuck and you're feeling better."

"Perhaps." Ana would have to check the weather reports. If there was a slight chance that they would be free to leave in the morning, she would be the first one out of there.

"Get some rest then..." Ciara spotted someone coming up behind Ana. "Or perhaps you had something more... rigorous...in mind?"

Ana turned to find Rhys striding toward them, the expression on his face inscrutable. He barely spared Ciara a glance as he hooked his hand around her arm and dragged her away with a guttural, "Excuse us."

They barely made it a few feet down the hall before he spun her around to look at him. "What the hell was that?"

"What?"

"You just ditched me back there."

That was the idea. Obviously it hadn't worked. "I want to be alone, Rhys."

He refused to let her go when she tried to wrench her arm from his grip. "Alone. Is that what you truly want? Or are you rushing to be with someone else?"

Ana glared at him. "You have *got* to be kidding me."

"There's someone else, isn't there?" he growled.

In a manner of speaking, there was, but she wasn't about to tell him anything. "Let go, Rhys."

He pushed her against the wall, partially hiding them from prying eyes with a large potted plant. Gripping her upper arms, he snarled, "If you think that anyone else can make you feel the way I can, you're wrong."

"I don't feel anything for you." She put her hand up when he started to argue. "I did once. I won't deny that. And I might have a few residual…issues…that need to be resolved, but things have changed. I've changed. It took me a long time to pull myself back together again and if that means there's someone else in my life then you're just going to have to suck it up and move on. Especially since it would be your fault there's someone else in the first place."

The muscles in his jaw tensed, and Ana braced herself for an argument, but he let her go.

"It was never meant to be forever."

"I didn't get the memo." She shoved him back. "I've moved on, so should you."

He studied her for a long moment. "I want to meet him."

"Who?" Ana knew exactly who he meant.

"The guy you're with."

How had things gotten so blown out of proportion? The idea that Rhys wanted to meet this mythical person made her want to laugh. It was so ludicrous, she had to ask, "You want to meet him? For what purpose? To scare him away?"

"To vet him. To see who's replaced me."

He was serious. This was spiraling out of control way too

quickly. Ana shook her head. "You are out of your mind. First of all, this guy you're talking about is a figment of your imagination." She didn't have to look too hard to see the relief wash over him. "But that doesn't mean I want you in my life, either."

Annoyance crept back into his features. "Ana...I know I can't make up for the time we lost. But what we had was good. We both know that. It wouldn't take much to pick up from where we left off."

He really had no idea, did he?

"Rhys." She cupped his face and stared him straight in the eyes. "It destroyed me when I thought you were dead. It changed me. I'm not the same woman anymore. I can't go back again."

His eyes were pleading. "Ana, I just want the chance to make it up to you."

And he thought he could do that during their time there? "You do realize I won't see you again outside of this hotel. So what's the point?"

Rhys appeared to be momentarily stunned by her remark. It really hadn't occurred to him that she wouldn't welcome him with open arms when she found out he wasn't dead.

"What did you think was going to happen, Rhys? That I would get one look at you and go rushing back into your arms?"

From the expression on his face, that was exactly what he'd thought.

Chapter Six

Rhys stared at Ana. He had imagined their reunion a million times and in every scenario she was overjoyed to see him and, needless to say, they would end up expressing that joy in many creative ways.

Not once did it occur to him that she would be so hurt by what he had done.

He was such a fucking asshole.

Of course she would be hurt and angry. It had been two years when, in his mind, he was only going to be gone a few days. A week or two at most. She'd thought him dead. Had grieved him. And, as much as he hated to admit it, had gotten over him.

Rhys took another half step back. "Ana…I get it and I'm sorry. It was never a well thought out plan. All I knew at the time was that I needed to protect you and I took the chance to do it when I thought it was the only way. I did it without thinking of the consequences."

No, he hadn't. He had been too busy thinking about his feelings and his needs that he had completely overlooked hers.

Gazing into her eyes now, Rhys saw the devastation he had wrought and it tore through him with jagged claws and left him shredded. Raw. But not nearly as devastated as she was.

"I'd like the chance to make it right…" His words died at the withering glare she gave him. "But I'm thinking that there's no way I can do that."

Gritting his teeth, he forced himself back a little more. As much as he hated to say it, he had fucked up and in doing so, he'd extinguished the one shining light he saw at the end of the tunnel.

That he had thought he, Rhys Stone, would walk off into the sunset and live happily ever after. What a fucking joke. Nothing in his life had ever gone the way it was supposed to. What made him think this would? When he and Ana had found each other two years previously, there had been a glimmer of hope. Clearly, over their time apart, he had built up a fantasy in his head, had counted on it, only to now find out it had been ruined by his own hand. His own arrogance.

Because he wanted to break something, he clenched his hands into tight fists and grunted a goodbye before stalking away.

He rounded the corner and straight into a crowd of people. Rhys didn't even slow down. He simply plowed through the throng and ignored the gasps and scornful remarks. If they wanted to make an issue, he would welcome it. He could use a good fight. Though it was highly unlikely, considering the type of people staying at the hotel. There would be more chance of a lawsuit than anything.

Nothing that would satisfy his need for a physical release.

Rhys soon found himself at the recreation center, looking for an outlet for his frustration.

There was one place he could think of going – the gym.

Not caring that he wasn't wearing workout clothes, Rhys found the nearest punching bag, tore off his sweater to leave him in trousers and a T-shirt, and sought to thoroughly beat the hell out of it.

He alternated strikes using his fists, elbows, knees and feet to systematically work off the tension and anger.

Rhys had no idea how long it took him, but by the time his muscles ached and sweat was dripping off him, he finally felt calm enough to stop.

Using his sweater as a towel, he mopped the sweat from his face and arms. It was then that he noticed he had gathered quite the crowd of women who watched him with a mix of awe and obvious lust. None, of course, was the one woman he wanted.

Ignoring their stares and attempts to stop him for conversation, he made his way back up to the penthouse.

As relaxed and spent as his body was, Rhys' mind was still reeling. Most of the thoughts had to do with Ana. There was no getting around that. Once he'd seen her again, Rhys had known that he would be preoccupied with her. How could he not? Ana was—always would be—the love of his life.

Only now he had to get used to the idea that she wanted nothing to do with him.

Rhys shoved the thought aside. As much as it hurt him—and he knew it would drive him crazy—at the moment he couldn't afford to let himself get derailed.

Work now. Losing his shit over the loss of his dream woman later.

What was so ironic was that all the effort he was putting into his work was now pointless without her waiting for him on the other end. Wasn't a quiet life with Ana what he was working so hard to attain in the first place?

Fuck.

He had to sort out his priorities and work through them, focusing his attention on one thing at a time. Otherwise, he'd never survive this without turning into a gibbering wreck.

If deluding himself into believing he could talk Ana around once this was all done was what he had to do, then he'd do it.

He took a long, hot shower as he tried to get his head back in gear. Rhys was here for one thing and, until Ana had shocked the determination out of his head with her surprise appearance, he'd had a plan.

All he had to do now was get his head on straight and execute it.

As he toweled off his resolve returned. His focus.

There would be nothing that could stand in his way.

Ana crept into the dark gallery. Memorizing her steps during her earlier visit helped her navigate. Meanwhile, the details about the security measures she'd gotten from the night guard gave her a boost of confidence. While most of the hotel's patrons were having nightcaps and getting ready for bed, she had grilled a young staff member. A smile and a bat of her lashes had gotten him to give up everything he knew about the subject.

The one thing she couldn't quite figure out was the case itself. Ana needed a good look at it so she could figure out a workaround. Without people getting in her way, she would at least have that chance.

But if she was caught in there now...

Ana was prepared to take the risk. The sooner she figured the security out, the sooner she could make a plan. Then the moment the snow let up, she would get the hell out of there and back to her life.

She shoved aside the niggling realization that Rhys wasn't going to be a part of that. Getting over the fact that he had lied was one on a list of issues she had. Ana was glad Rhys was alive, truly. Only, she wasn't sure how he fit into her life now. There was too much that had changed, that was now organized just so.

The truth was, Ana didn't want him showing up and destroying the status quo of her life as he had already done to her state of mind.

Now there was the added challenge of getting things back to normal after all this, Ana wasn't sure if she could take much more.

Adding Rhys to the mix was too dangerous. Maybe not in the way Rhys thought she was in danger, but for her carefully reconstructed life and peace of mind.

Even now, she was so busy thinking about him, she nearly tripped an alarm by skirting too close to the mesmerizing fist-sized emeralds.

Focus, Ana.

How utterly ridiculous would it be if she tripped the

sensors on a recon mission when she went out of her way to perform the much more complicated task of altering the security camera feed?

Ana stepped away from the pressure plates that had been installed at the bases of the podiums. Whoever set up the room was smart. The seemingly random placement of the displays meant that the security measures overlapped on the more valuable pieces. Not that they were lacking on any of the others.

It was a work of art, really. But nothing was more beautiful to her than her target.

Ana studied the casing and logically worked through the different possibilities. Even though it had been a couple of years, the cogs of her old self began to fall back into place.

Sure they were a little rusty, but they were working.

The adrenaline, the thrill of doing the illicit, wasn't a feeling she'd forgotten. It was what kept her addicted to her job—that life—from the very first.

Still, Ana couldn't let herself get caught up. She had more important things to worry about.

This was the last trip into her old life. Ana would make doubly sure of it this time.

But could she really do that? She never could have anticipated that Marco Valente would storm into her carefully peaceful life and turn it inside out so easily and thoroughly.

Once upon a time, they had worked together on a few jobs where their combined talents had been needed. She had been there to undermine security while he was a demolitions man who'd turned out to be as unstable as the explosives he used.

The 'agency' that they worked for liked to mix and match the crews according to need and ability. All that mattered was that the job got done. It didn't matter that among the pool of talent was the occasional psycho.

And that was what Marco turned out to be.

At first, he was the new guy, the one no one had worked

with before, so it went without saying that there had been an adjustment period. Strangely enough, however, the more they'd worked with him, the less he'd meshed with anyone.

It wasn't long before Marco had been skipped over in favor of other more cooperative and reliable members of the agency with a similar skill set, leading him to slowly disappear from the scene.

That was until a few days ago when she'd received a text in the middle of the night to check her email. The heavily encrypted one from an anonymous sender.

Ana had looked and found photos of her home, of her, of her son. In what she'd thought was their safe and secluded home. Along with them came a promise to blow it all to hell if she didn't do as he'd asked.

What was she supposed to do?

She didn't have a choice.

So she had called one of the few people she trusted who was, ironically enough, a con artist. Javier Bolivar was smart, skilled and a good friend that had had her back more than once over the years.

He'd sworn to guard Eric with his life until she returned. And Ana knew he would.

If only she could count on everyone to do as they promised.

But she wasn't thinking about Rhys right now.

Glaring at the case holding the diamond, she pursed her lips as she worked out a way of getting it out without tripping any sensors. It would take some problem solving, but Ana was confident she would get around the security. She merely needed the time to figure it out.

A soft shuffling sound tore her from her near meditative state and she stiffened instinctively as she listened.

Someone else was in there with her.

Chapter Seven

Rhys was mildly surprised when he checked the monitoring of the gallery and found that someone had tampered with the feed. It saved him a job, but also left him wondering who else was there to liberate a few jewels.

It wasn't a stretch to the imagination that there would be quite a few thieves there to try to steal a gem or two. It was basically a glittering buffet waiting to be plundered. Whoever came up with the idea to mix a gem exhibition and one of the biggest social events on the calendar probably thought themselves a marketing genius. What they'd actually done was create a must-attend, weeklong smorgasbord for any number of criminals — cons, thieves, someone out to make a name for themselves… The list was endless.

Security probably thought they had a lock on everything, but it was obvious from the surveillance being compromised alone that they were in over their heads.

Still, he wasn't about to look a gift horse in the mouth. Because it had been tampered with, he knew two things — he wouldn't be seen, and there was someone else there. Someone who was skilled and quite possibly as dangerous.

Rhys slipped on a pair of innocuous-appearing glasses. He didn't know how the boys in tech did it, but they always managed to come up with something that wowed him. This time around, they'd provided him with a pair that might as well have been magical eyes for all they could do.

He entered the gallery from a side entrance after dealing with the simple lock. He wondered how anyone thought anything was secure when the advent of keycards made things that much easier for people to gain access to places they weren't supposed to be in.

Hotel staff were reigned by rules and ethics, whereas anyone else not burdened by the same qualms could find the entire hotel at their disposal. Something as simple as a misplaced access card carried by a cleaner or security could easily be used to clone another. Which was exactly what he'd done the first night he'd been there.

Had anyone else come up with the same idea?

Rhys would imagine there would be at least one or two others. He had half a mind to put together a brief and leave it for the hotel so they could shore up their tactics when dealing with special events. The security for the hotel in general was quite good. He was actually impressed by it. It took a great deal of skill, the right equipment and training to compromise the cameras and clone cards. It was whoever dealt with the exhibition that Rhys had an issue with.

A quick scan of the room told him very little. It wasn't until he'd switched the glasses to thermal that he saw a figure skulking around the outskirts of the room. And another standing in the middle of the room as if they had no care in the world.

They had some bollocks, that was for sure.

Unsure of what to be more concerned about, Rhys studied them for a moment. The one in the heart of the gallery simply stood and studied the gem in the case in front of them.

But the other one... That blur of red, yellow and green crept around the perimeter toward the other.

Were they working together?

It was a possibility that evaporated when the one doing the creeping pulled out a gun.

They were going to take the other out as simply as that?

Rhys was both stunned and amused at the idiocy. At the very least, it would mean one less asshole to compete with. That was, if their stupidity didn't get the entire exhibit put on lockdown. That wouldn't be too great. Rhys started edging toward them, fully intending on taking them out before he or she could ruin all his work for the past couple of years.

That was until he turned his gaze back to the one in front of the case. The cross-armed pose the figure had adopted had changed. It was a woman. That much was clear in the stance. Weight on one leg, arms not crossed now, but wound around her middle as she thought.

Much like he had found Ana earlier…

Realization stopped his heart for an instant before it thundered to life again.

Damn it! It *was* Ana!

Heart galloping, Rhys gave up stealth for speed and dashed around the pedestals. What the hell was she doing in there? And totally oblivious to the danger she was in.

Just as the shadow was within a few feet of her, she reacted. She incapacitated and disarmed her adversary in quick, quiet succession, stopping Rhys dead where he stood. With a strange sense of pride, Rhys observed her. Now that the would-be assailant was down and not a threat, she dragged them to a dark corner of the room, took their weapon and disappeared.

He knew he had a dumbfounded smile on his face. Ana certainly checked the well-trained box. So why was she there?

Stupid question, really. She was obviously there for the diamond, just like every other asshole was.

Just like he was.

But that didn't answer everything. Why would Ana want to steal a diamond?

When they had first met, she'd told him she was an artist traveling and working her way through Europe looking for inspiration. Not a countess and certainly not a thief. But then what did he actually know about her?

Rhys only knew what she had shared with him. That, and the chemistry between them, rivaled the burn of the sun. Blistering and relentless, it had scorched away all thought and left consideration for everything else by the wayside.

And it had cost him the life of his partner.

Guilt over that fact weighed heavily on him. But he was so close now to getting retribution. Days away. With the diamond, he could end it all for the bastard who had killed his partner and subsequently taken him from Ana for the past couple of years.

It wouldn't be as sweet as putting a bullet in his skull, but Rhys wasn't going to be choosy. He wanted it done and over with so he could finally move on with his life. Then he could find Ana again and settle down.

He had managed to find her, accidentally — not that it mattered. Now all he had to figure out was a way to convince her that the rest was a good idea.

Not wanting to hang around, Rhys backtracked to the door he'd entered through.

As he made his way through the halls, he wondered if any of the people vying for the diamond actually knew what they were really after.

The diamond on its own was worth a fortune, but it was what was hidden on it that was the real prize.

Unbeknownst to many, etched into the edges of the massive diamond was a formula for a devastating new drug. One that would make whoever possessed it billions of dollars.

All it would cost was the lives of the users.

Rhys couldn't let it get into the wrong hands. Especially not the hands of the murdering psycho who he'd been hunting the past twenty-four months.

Which brought a question to mind — what side of the line did Ana fall on?

He intended to find out.

Before long, Rhys found himself in front of her door once again, only this time he decided to knock.

It took moments before he heard her soft footfalls on the other side. Rhys stood in full view of the peephole so she could see it was him. He lifted his hands and did a slow turn, pulling up the back of his shirt so she could see he wasn't hiding anything.

The door opened a crack to reveal a sliver of her face.

"What do you want, Rhys?"

"To make sure you're okay after what I saw go down in the gallery."

The door parted a little more as her expressive eyes widened. She narrowed them and the door menacingly. "I don't know what you're talking about."

"Cut the crap, Ana, and let me in." He looked up and down the silent hall meaningfully then met her gaze again. "Unless you want me to make a scene and bring the nice security guard back up here again."

The door closed on an oath and quickly reopened. "Come on, then."

She backed up as he walked in, letting him close the door while she eyed him warily.

It wasn't like he was going to bite. Well, not if she didn't want him to.

Rhys kept walking, forcing her backward into the suite toward the living area since she wasn't about to let him get close.

"So tell me again why a countess would be here for the Winter Ball at the same time as a jewelry exhibition seemingly obsessed with a diamond while at the same time conveniently equipped for repelling indoors." He put up his hand when she started to protest. "Don't bullshit me. I know what outdoor climbing equipment looks like." He'd used it enough times to know the difference at a glance.

Ana backed into a wall and glowered at him, refusing to answer but letting him continue.

"Then I find you staring at the same diamond in the exhibit more than a few times, once after hours, in the dark, after somehow getting around some very sophisticated security."

Rhys pressed his palms against the wall on either side of her head. The action caged her in, but he knew, as she did, that she could get away from him whenever she wanted.

She didn't budge. "Why are you keeping such a close eye on me, Rhys?" She smirked as realization spread clearly over her face. "Or are you keeping tabs on the diamond?"

"I'm the one asking the questions, Ana."

She tipped her chin up a notch. "And I'm not answering until I get a few from you."

Rhys sighed. All the muscles in his body seemed to tense at the thought of baring his soul to her. He would if he thought she would reciprocate and if he believed she could handle it.

He wasn't sure he trusted her on either count.

But she was right. A little exchange of information wasn't too much to ask.

Though, what to tell her?

What *could* he tell her?

Rhys stepped back and motioned for her to sit on the plush-looking sofa. After a moment of hesitation, she did, surprising him.

When he saw her hand slide briefly under a cushion, as if she was checking for something, the surprise turned to irritation. "What do you have under there?"

Ana pursed her lips and shoved the pillow aside to reveal a wicked-looking blade gleaming in the light.

"Are you kidding me? I'm not going to hurt you. On the table." So she was careful and prepared. And she didn't trust him.

That caused an ache deep in his chest.

"I came to talk. You won't need that or whatever else you've got hidden around here."

"I'd rather be safe than sorry." She placed the blade delicately on the table in front of her. Within reach, if she needed it.

Rhys let it be. "I am watching the diamond. I'm planning on stealing it."

It amused him a tiny bit to see her jaw slacken.

"You're a thief?"

"When duty calls for it. The people I work for like to think that their motives are more altruistic, or at least they word it better."

He watched the emotions play on her face, morphing quickly one to another, before she finally said, "You're a spy."

Rhys didn't deny it. "And if I am correct, *you're* the thief."

She leaned back but didn't argue against it either. "If you want the diamond you'd better work fast before someone steals it out from under your nose."

It was obvious she meant she would be the one to best him.

Not if he had anything to say about it. Rhys didn't let it faze him, however. In fact, that she was being so forthcoming was encouraging.

Rhys dropped onto the other end of the couch and curled a knee up on it. Relaxed, comfortable, as if they were doing nothing more than chatting about the weather.

Her heart rattled in her chest like a convict trying to get free. Finally, they were getting somewhere. So he was a… what? A spy? A con. What she knew for sure was that he couldn't be trusted.

He'd been lying to her from the beginning, so what was to stop him from continuing to do so now?

Simply because he said he wanted to get things out in the open didn't mean a thing. They were only words. Hollow, meaningless words.

Hadn't life already shown her how truly empty they could be?

So she would listen, assess, and deliberate over his words, but she didn't have to believe them.

Just like she wouldn't have to say a single thing she didn't want to.

What she did have to do was figure out his plan for getting the diamond and beat him, and everyone else, to it. Ana was curious, however, as to why everyone seemed to be after that particular gem. It was a diamond. A huge one, sure, but to be the prize for so many? There had to be more that she didn't know.

It wasn't like her to jump straight into a job without doing a little background work, but seeing as Marco hadn't given her much of a choice, she had agreed and dived in without a second thought.

Her stomach rolled at the thought of Marco harming a hair on Eric's head. She knew he had no compunction against harming anyone, not even children, especially if he knew it would get his point across. If he didn't get what he wanted, he would do whatever it took to make his displeasure known in the most terrible way.

What was more terrible than hurting her baby?

Rhys forgotten for the moment, Ana fought to calm the roiling in her stomach, the rising panic. She wouldn't be any good to anyone if she couldn't keep it together and get the job done.

"Hey."

A squeeze of her hand brought her back to reality. Ana found Rhys staring at her intently, a grip on both her hands.

"What happened? You just checked out on me." The concern on his face was clear. But was it real?

"I'm fine." She tugged her hands out of his and scooted farther back against the armrest.

Rhys watched her a while longer. His piercing coal black eyes studied her in a way that she could almost feel him inside her head.

Breaking eye contact, Ana got up. "Want a drink?"

Her attempt at changing the subject didn't go undetected, but he nodded. "Water, thanks."

Ana was thinking the same thing. She needed to stay focused, but she also had to get away from his scrutiny, if only for a few seconds.

She headed to the kitchen and retrieved a couple of bottles of mineral water from the fridge. On a whim, Ana also pulled out a cheese platter and some handmade gourmet chocolates that had come complimentary with the suite. She was hungry. If he was as well, he was welcome to join her, but Ana couldn't care less either way.

She handed him his bottle then set the food on the table as she settled back in her seat.

An almost wistful expression briefly came over his face while he stared at the meager offering. She was reminded as well to their time back in Positano when they would get by on scraps of food because they'd been unwilling to leave their little sanctuary unless it had been absolutely necessary.

They'd subsisted mainly on whatever scraps they'd been able to put together from the meals they'd brought back, meager grocery shopping, and on sex.

In other words, they had been complete idiots.

What else would happen when they let their hormones control them? Ana pinched a decadent-looking chocolate and placed it on her tongue to let it melt.

Rhys eyed the table a little longer before taking a sip from his bottle.

"I didn't poison it, if that's what you're worried about." Ana tried to hide the amusement from her words but couldn't completely.

"I wasn't worried." Rhys still didn't take anything. Instead he, turned his gaze to watch her — intently.

"What?"

"I was just thinking back. Kind of hard not to after seeing you again after all this time."

Too much time. Ana shrugged.

He held her gaze levelly. "You can't say that seeing me hasn't brought back a flood of memories."

"I never put them aside. They've been with me, always." It was a fact that she didn't bother to try to elaborate.

His face softened. "Ana…"

"If you're going to apologize for your disappearing act, you can save your breath. It's fine. It's done and over with."

Anger flashed in his eyes. "Not to me it isn't."

The thoughts whirling around his mind were clear on his face as he tried to formulate an argument.

"Really. Don't bother. Nothing you say will change anything. What happened, happened."

He clenched his fists then opened and closed them. "I'm more worried about figuring out what happens now. Next."

"As far as I'm concerned, we should just go our separate ways." Ana tried to force a smile but barely managed a grim line.

"I'm part of that equation too, don't forget. You can't discount my say. I think we should try—"

Ana put up her hand. "Did you think about my say when you did what you did?"

His expression contrite, he held her gaze. "I was thinking it was the best *for* you."

"But I had absolutely no say." There was a clutch in her chest. How different things would have been if he had only talked to her. "Maybe I think this is the best for *you*. You said it yourself. You're no thief."

Rhys growled something under his breath as he raked his hands through his hair. "I deserve that. But we owe it to ourselves to sort this out." He waved a hand between them.

"Sort what out? As far as I'm concerned, what we had died the night you did."

"Like hell." Rhys leaned in closer. "You still want me."

Ana felt something that closely resembled panic flutter in her gut, so she armored herself with anger. Anger at being left alone. At being abandoned.

"You have some gall. Just because you've miraculously come back from the grave, I'm supposed to do a happy dance and jump straight back into bed with you?"

He let his gaze wander over her. "The thought of getting naked with you again is the one driving force that kept me going these past couple of years."

She gritted her teeth against the flare of awareness that the look in his eyes ignited. "And you never thought that death might have been a bit too final? If you needed to get away from me you could have said so. Letting me think you were dead was cruel."

When he tried to argue, she shoved him back. "I was alone, Rhys. Terrified, alone, and devastated. I grieved for you, for months. There were days where I couldn't even get out of bed. And when I did, I would cry myself sick." It had been a few months before she'd realized that the nausea hadn't all been because of the crying. Ana narrowed her eyes at him. "You have no idea what you put me through."

He closed his hands over her shoulders. Rhys was close enough now that she could see the bleak devastation in his eyes as he remembered that period of time as well. "You think it was easy for me? Walking away from you was the hardest thing I ever had to do. Somehow I found the balls to do it. To keep you safe."

"You keep saying that, but it's pretty hollow when you won't tell me what you're keeping me safe from."

For a long moment, he glared at her. She could almost see him dismissing arguments in his head. Finally, he took a deep breath. "You know what I do now and you can obviously take care of yourself."

"You would have known that a lot sooner if you hadn't have run off."

He gave her a withering glance before he turned away. "My partner was killed in that explosion. He'd stayed close, wanting to keep an eye on me. To keep me safe. It was my fault he was there and vulnerable. Not to mention the fact that it had happened so close to you, as well…"

Ana searched his eyes and saw that what he said was true. Stunned, she waited for him to continue.

"We were in the area to do some reconnaissance."

"I was there for work, too."

He nodded. "I figured. What is it you do again?"

Rhys' eyes had lost that haunted, wary expression when he looked at her now. Instead, there was a hint of amusement. Ana went with it. It was a relief, really. Anger and grief were draining.

"Let's just say I'm a specialist in problematic acquisitions."

His smirk grew at her admission. "All right, then. And what was proving so hard to get a hold of that they needed your expertise?"

"A painting. I had finally managed to obtain it the night before we…connected."

From the darkening of his eyes and the way he ran his tongue over his bottom lip, she knew he was thinking about that night as well.

It had been good. *They* had been good.

Spectacularly so.

Did she dare lose herself in him again? It was very tempting. That big body, the soulful eyes…

What was she thinking?

Ana silenced the voice in her head whispering suggestions about what she could do with that body. What it could do to hers…

"You seem angry again."

As much as she hated it, maybe she needed to stay angry to keep her from making another mistake.

"Where do you see this going, Rhys?"

"To your bed first. Then after all this is over, I had envisioned the happily-ever-after scenario. Marriage, kids, maybe even a picket fence." He hazarded a glance over at her. "If that's what you want, of course. If it's not, then I'd be happy to roll with whatever you do."

Why couldn't he have said this before he'd disappeared? Ana had wanted it all, too. Thought they would with the naïve, wishful thinking of a woman newly in love. But now? How could she have faith in a man she knew virtually nothing about?

Time to lay out her terms.

She wet her lips, easing into the conversation. "For me to even consider that I'd need to know everything about you."

His mouth thinned. "You know already everything about me that matters."

Ana shook her head. "I know that you and I were once

compatible in bed and that you can lie. That's not enough."

"I can prove that we still are compatible, in bed and out. And any lies I told you were for a good reason. But beyond that, you know who I am as a person. As a man." He peered into her eyes, daring her to say otherwise. "I bared my soul to you when we were together in Positano."

And she had done the same. The freedom of being herself, who she truly was, with someone had been amazing and probably contributed to the romance of the time there.

"It's not enough. Not for forever like you want. I don't know if I could give that to you. If I could give myself to you knowing that there are parts of you that are locked away."

"It's not like you aren't hiding things yourself."

Ana's heart froze. What did he know? "You already know what I do for a living. That's about as sordid as my life gets." If he knew anything more, she hoped that would get him talking.

She sensed his inner turmoil as he asked, "What do you plan to do once you leave the life behind?"

Hadn't she already tried that? And failed miserably? "I'm not sure that ever happens."

"I never imagined you would be a pessimist." Rhys smiled softly. "Life is what you make of it. What you craft it into."

And the life she had made for herself had been carefully constructed. Every detail had been agonized over to maximize the chances of her living a quiet, normal life and yet here she was.

"I can tell you all the planning in the world doesn't always work out the way you imagine."

"Don't I know it." The scowl on his face mirrored what was going on in her head.

So now what? Where did all this talk leave them? By her reckoning, they were in the exact same spot as when they'd started talking. She wasn't willing to risk it all again for him and he still wasn't telling her enough to even contemplate it.

And then there was the danger that he was reluctant to talk about. Ana had enough of that in her life without him adding to it.

Still, the thought that he considered her weak and in need of his protection bothered her. Ana had been through more than he could imagine. Much of which would probably make him squirm in his seat for ever assuming that she was in need of his so-called protection.

"If you knew that I've faced down insane men, weapons of just about every caliber, and defied some immense odds, would you have told me what was going on with you?"

To his credit, Rhys considered her words, actually appeared to be thinking about them before he answered. "I don't know. It's instinct to want to protect the one you care about. Even if they are capable of handling pretty much anything. I would have done whatever it took to keep you safe."

He kept saying it. Like a mantra that he truly believed. Ana tried to look at it from his point of view and she could understand where he was coming from. However, it didn't negate the hurt and the loneliness and the sheer pain of what he'd put her though.

But she understood why he had done it.

Ana found herself wishing they could go back and start all over again. On the other hand, if he kept secrets it would make it easier to keep hers from him as well.

"Rhys…"

He knew what was coming, she could see it on his face. But, true to form, he wasn't about to sit back and take it.

"I don't want to hear it. I definitely don't want to hear you to tell me to fuck off. And if you try to let me down easy, I'm going to lose my shit."

She waved at the door. "Then save us both the aggravation and just go."

Rhys only shook his head. "Not when I know we're good together."

Ana glared at him. "Maybe once…"

"Don't give me that bullshit again. You and I both know that it could be the same now if you'd give us a chance."

"Why can't you just admit you screwed up and let me live my life?"

His temper whipped her like a lash, stirring her own. "I have admitted it. But I'm not about to let you go. Not again. Not straight after I've found you again."

She shoved him when he tried to get closer. "Just leave."

He cupped her cheek. The anguish at the thought of leaving her dulled his eyes. "I can't."

Chapter Eight

Rhys gave her a split second to pull away. Ana knew she had a choice and when she didn't take it, she knew there was no stopping the insane passion that blistered between them.

Dragging her toward him, Rhys rolled her under him at the same time attacking her mouth with a fervor that matched hers.

The taste of him, his scent, were just as she remembered. He was right when he'd said they were good together. That there wouldn't be anyone else that could even come close to what he did to her. Rhys was ingrained in her.

Ana dragged him closer, shoving her hands under his shirt so she could touch and feel his warm skin as well as the play of the hard muscles beneath.

How many times had she imagined doing this? So many nights she'd spent longing to be able to touch him again. To feel Rhys. To taste him.

The reality of it was intoxicating. Much better than it had been in her dreams. Even though her senses were rioting — rejoicing — there was a chunk of her heart that wept. The conflicting emotions threatened to drive her insane. So she gave in to the most powerful.

Ana let the flames burn. Invited them to engulf her.

Tugging his clothes off, Ana could only think of seeing him, feeling him. Single-mindedly, she worked at the buttons. Once she managed to get his shirt off, she ran her hands over his heated skin. There were scars. She followed the trail of one she remembered well. He'd told her he had been in some sort of accident, but knowing what she did now and seeing how many more he had added over the past couple of years, a frisson of fear lanced through her.

As if intuiting what she was thinking, Rhys pulled her hands away, dragging them up to his neck instead. Ana tunneled them into his hair, pulling him down to meet her mouth again.

The electricity that came from the barest touch of his lips against hers was nothing compared to the charge she got when he brushed her tongue with his. Ana couldn't stop herself from arching under his hands when he rucked her clothes up and out of the way to have unhindered access to her breasts.

She moaned a string of unintelligible sounds as he drew the hard tip of one into his mouth and laved it with his tongue before sucking gently. The sensation lanced through her, sapping the strength from her muscles then pooled low in her pelvis.

Again, completely in tune with her, Rhys slipped a hand down her side to unbutton her trousers and pushed them down so he could delve his fingers between her thighs. Legs and arms trapped in her clothes, Ana could do nothing but let him.

Not that it occurred to her to even try to stop him.

Rhys, obviously pleased she was going to let him do what he liked, took full advantage. He explored her with his hands, his mouth, his tongue, driving her slowly, inexorably mad with each heated caress.

She'd missed this—him. No one could do the same thing to her senses as Rhys. Not that there had been that many to compare to him. Before and definitely not after. She had been like a widow in mourning. There had been no time, no emotion, to waste on someone who wasn't Rhys.

But the reality of him back in her arms, pressed skin to skin to her, blasted everything else out of her mind.

Ana wrestled her top until she freed her arms and tore it off. At last, she could touch him too and drive him as crazy as he was driving her. Running her nails down his back, she was rewarded with a hiss from him. Then a bite on her shoulder.

What flowed between them was primal, elemental. Unstoppable.

Shimmying out of her trousers, she wrapped one leg around his lean hip and anchored him closer and rubbed her breasts against his rough chest. As she writhed, the light sprinkling of hair abraded her sensitive flesh wonderfully, sending sparks of awareness through her.

"We need a bed." The words were groaned into her throat though he didn't seem to have any more inclination to stop what they were doing and move than she.

"Do we?" She could recall many occasions where they hadn't had one and they'd made out perfectly fine.

More than.

He groaned when she gave him a mirroring nip on the shoulder. "We can make our way there." Another groan when she flicked her tongue over his nipple. "Eventually."

Sounded good to her.

Ana gripped his head with both hands, cutting off any chance of further conversation by pressing her mouth to his. He tasted of coffee and the wicked promises that Rhys didn't have to articulate. That she knew he would make good on.

His physique was leaner than she remembered. Rhys was still well muscled but her fingers could clearly trace each and every one now. His body certainly told her he'd been through a rough couple of years.

Her own had changed significantly as well, though he didn't seem to notice. Rhys greedily explored her form, as if it was the only sustenance his body needed. Craved.

Ana could definitely understand the feeling. The reality of him being alive and in her arms again was a heady thing. She could still hardly believe it.

She arched, pressing as much of herself against him as she could. There was no telling how long they would have together this time — if there would even be a next time — so

Ana was determined to make the most of it.

He pulled back then, using her leg to bring her up with him. Rhys sat up, giving her a chance to straddle him as he lavished attention on her breasts.

The pleasure of his touch spread through her body, heating her up. The molten ache at the apex of her thighs grew with each mounting second until she couldn't—wouldn't—wait any longer.

Ana slipped a hand between them to grip his erection. Grazing the tip with her thumb, she swiped the little bead of pre-cum that had collected there and used it to slick the head of his cock. Taking his grunt into her mouth, Ana slowly began to rock, using the ridge of his cock to pleasure herself.

Teasing him when they were both so on edge was a dangerous game. One that she knew would pay off very well.

His muscles bunched and the tension in him built.

Then she pulled out of the kiss, sucking his bottom lip on the way back. The nip she gave him made Rhys' control snap.

He wrapped an arm around her before he curved his hand under her ass and lifted her, bringing her down on his cock as he angled it with his other. The slow slide down his body as he filled her exponentially intensified the pleasure exploding in Ana. As if he couldn't wait any longer, Rhys bucked his hips to get inside her as deeply and as quickly as he could with one hard thrust.

Ana couldn't breathe. The stretch, the way he fit so perfectly inside her, was sublime.

Rhys didn't give her a chance to dwell. Gripping her hips, he rocked her in counterpoint to his thrusts. Each time he pulled back, the thick veined ridge of him sent ripples of sensation fluttering through her.

Then the plunge back in would do the same, but with the added bonus of hitting a spot deep inside that multiplied the pleasure.

When he brought his fingers into play and circled her clit, Ana was lost.

A keening cry on her lips, Ana gripped him to her as pleasure slammed into her.

"I've missed that sound." Rhys had slowed his thrusts, though he smiled now as she pulsed around him.

The smug look on his face through the foggy haze set off a twinge of annoyance. He'd made her come so easily. Ana was determined to bring him to his knees next.

Grinning, she leaned in to graze his earlobe with her teeth and whispered, "Let's see if I can get you to make that sound I've missed so much."

"Not before we find a bed." Still embedded inside her, Rhys stood and started a slow walk toward the bedroom.

Ana wrapped her legs around him but wasn't about to let him off that easily. Rhythmically tightening her muscles around his cock, she bounced a little, working herself up and down his erection.

"God, Ana." His steps faltered and he turned to press her against the wall. "Play fair."

She wriggled as much as he would allow.

Rhys' breathing was uneven, his body trembling under the strain of trying to hold his climax off.

Too bad for him Ana knew how to work his body as well as he knew hers.

Ana grazed his shoulder with her teeth, nibbling a path up to his ear. She flicked her tongue over the lobe just before she bit.

He pulled back to study her, as if he were afraid he'd never see her again. Ana knew that this went beyond merely sating their lust. Even if she wasn't willing to admit it.

Rhys said nothing as he peered into her eyes. He closed his hands around her hips and let go of his control. With a growl, he hefted her up and rocked back until he almost completely slipped from her body. On an oath, he pushed himself back in. Rhys kissed her deeply as he thrust in an ever-quickening rhythm that had her rushing toward orgasm again.

This time, not without him.

Rhys plunged into her like a madman galloping toward a cliff. He had wanted to reconnect with her, and sex was definitely a big part of his plans, but he had wanted it to be soft and slow. To make up for lost time. He should have known better. The fire between them burned too hot to control.

And her speedy orgasm had proven to him just how much she had missed him as well. That he had managed to keep from coming at that point was a miracle. He wanted to get her somewhere comfortable so he could spend as much time as he liked exploring her. But, when Ana was determined to get something, there was no stopping her.

Why would he want to?

The scent of her wound itself around him almost as tangibly as her limbs. Though he was able to recall her taste at will, the reality of being able to experience Ana again was almost too much.

She tightened around him, a sure sign she was close to orgasm. This time he had little choice. When Ana bit his lip, the little spike of pain and the naughty smile she gave him had him teetering on the edge.

But not before he felt her come around him again.

As much as he hated to put any distance between then, Rhys pulled back to give his hand some space. The added bonus being able to watch himself sliding in and out of her as he toyed with her clit with his thumb.

It took moments, but the monumental concentration it required for him not to give in before her had his body screaming for release.

Then at last, Ana's eyes glazed over. Her head dropped back against the wall and his name was cried out from her lips.

Feeling her clenching and fluttering around his cock was ecstasy and agony all at once, leaving him helpless to stop the inevitable.

Rhys pressed himself close once again, not wanting anything between them, and thrust into her, relishing her cries of excitement as he pushed himself as deeply he could into her tight, hot body over and over until he exploded.

His vision went white. The sensation was transcendent. He came again and again until his entire being was sapped of strength.

It was a long time before he could open his eyes. Miraculously, he had not only managed to keep upright, but still had Ana pressed to the wall.

Rhys never wanted to be anywhere else. If he could spend the rest of his life naked with Ana he'd go to the grave a happy man. Hell, if she would let him simply be a part of her life he'd be delighted.

What a sad state he was in.

Even so, he was reluctant to release her. The way she so sweetly clung to him, wrapped herself around him, he wasn't ready to break that connection.

Ana's sigh shifted her body against his ever so slightly, causing his to react. Obviously his body hadn't had its fill just yet. He couldn't blame himself. It had been a long time without her.

Without anyone.

He'd had no interest in anyone else while they'd been apart. Why would he when he was utterly consumed with getting revenge and he already had the perfect woman waiting for him at the end of it all?

He simply needed to convince her that he was just as suited to her.

Ana wriggled again and from the smirk on her face, she knew exactly what she was doing to him.

He couldn't stop himself from kissing her again. Leisurely now. Gently. They had all night now that the edge was off. He would make sure she knew what he had been dreaming about doing to her all the while they'd been apart.

As his cock hardened inside her once again, Ana couldn't help but smile. Round one had been particularly good. The subsequent ones would be better. She knew how easily they could lose track of time and end up in bed again for the next couple of months. Ana would indulge herself in him for this one night. There wasn't much else she could do anyway.

Might as well enjoy herself for a moment, no matter how fleeting it was.

The thought of parting ways once more lanced a shaft of pain through her. She shoved it ruthlessly aside. Later.

For a few hours, she was going to let herself be free.

Her body was still ultra-sensitized, so when he shifted, it was a close thing between too much and not enough. Ana decided it wasn't enough and added a few wriggles of her own. If this was going to be the last time they were together, she was going to make sure she got it all.

His passion, his power, and all the pleasure that would come from him unleashing all that.

Rhys groaned and kissed her deeply, teasing her with his tongue, letting her know exactly how languid he was feeling. The desperation, the raw need, was gone from the caress. What was there now was the simmering connection they'd always had between them.

When he drew back, there was a sleepy smirk on his face. "Are you going to let me take you to the bed now, or are we going to have another pit stop somewhere else?"

She laughed. "Depends on what strikes me along the way."

His answering chuckle was lost when he hefted her up and started walking. The brush of him against her, inside her, created a delicious friction that sparked tingles everywhere.

They made it to the bedroom this time without mishap, and Rhys rolled with her onto the bed until she was under him once again.

For a long while they lay entwined, kissing, exploring what skin they could reach without putting space between them, perfectly content just being connected. Being skin to skin with him was incredible. Feeling him deep inside her was even more so.

Ana rolled her hips experimentally, wanting to see what he would do in response. He thrust reflexively, once, then more solidly, effectively shutting down her ability to plan what to do next.

She bucked up, goading more movement from him until she lost herself in the rhythm and sensation of being utterly possessed by Rhys.

Being so close to him once again, reminded her of how good things were between them, at least sexually. Ana squealed with delight when he brought his hands into play.

Who was she kidding? They were great in and out of bed.

Rhys kept his gaze on hers, seemingly able to see every thought that flitted through her mind. Twisting to his side, he wound one of her legs over his hip. It freed up one arm so he could brush her hair out of her face and peer into her eyes.

The pace slowed then became languid and leisurely while, at the same time, the intensity and the sense of unity multiplied.

Mesmerized, Ana led him into oblivion.

Chapter Nine

Rhys woke feeling wonderfully loose and relaxed. That was until he reached over to the other side of the bed to find it cool.

All the rediscovered bliss evaporated.

"Ana?"

Anxiety gripped his heart in a vise. Where was she? Was she okay? Had someone broken in and gotten to her? Hurt her?

Untangling himself from the sheets and throwing them off, he leaped from the bed and rushed through to the living area.

Empty.

He headed back to the bedroom to get his clothes. If something had happened to Ana because of him, he'd never forgive himself.

On his way past the bathroom, her voice came to him from the other side of the door, and he sagged in immediate relief. At the urgent tone in her voice, he tensed again.

"I told you I'd get it and I will. I can't control the weather." Silence followed then a frustrated growl. "If I thought I could get it to you faster crawling through the snow, I would. But I can't. And you never thought to clue me in on how many people are interested in it. You didn't think that might complicate things? I was retired! A little head's up so I could prepare would have been nice!"

He heard her pacing, and he could almost feel her frustration through the door.

"I said I'd get it done. If you touch one hair on his head, I swear I'll hunt you down and gut you."

Rhys' heart stopped at her snarl then started to gallop. She was being coerced into stealing the diamond? Who did the mystery caller have who meant so much to her that she would give up retirement? Face jail time?

Who would inspire such devotion?

An ache developed in his chest that wouldn't be displaced. She had thought he was dead for the past two years. It was completely plausible that she had moved on with someone else.

So what the hell was she doing jumping into bed with him?

Rhys fought back the anger and the sense of betrayal. Ana had told him there was no one else. To be fair, it had taken a fair bit of coaxing to get that much out of her. So who was she doing this for? And how was he going to finesse the truth out of her?

Ana swore viciously before calling someone else.

"Javier, you have to do something. Marco isn't going to wait much longer and I'm stuck here until this snow lets up."

He was sure he heard her kicking something before continuing.

"I'm getting out of here as soon as possible, but you're going to have to figure something out because he's about to snap."

Rhys filed the names away for later along with all the new little details about her life. They certainly changed his opinion on what she was doing there.

She lowered her voice for the next few seconds, but when he heard his name, Rhys stepped closer to the door.

"Rhys doesn't need to know. Things are complicated enough. I don't need his help, Javi. Why? Because I don't need him in danger, as well. Don't you think I have enough to worry about?"

That warmed his heart. She wanted to keep him safe? After what he'd witnessed the night before, he knew she could take care of herself. But he never would have guessed she worried about his safety.

Knowing the last thing she would want was him barging in on her, he returned to the room. Rhys had managed to put his jeans back on when she strode in wearing a bathrobe, looking thoroughly annoyed.

Her eyes widened as if she were surprised to see him up and about. "Hey."

"Hey." He pulled on the rest of his clothes. "Up for some breakfast?"

She looked like she was on the verge of saying yes, but she hesitantly shook her head. "Rhys…"

"Don't say it." He stared her down. "I told you last night you're not going to push me away."

Ana pursed her lips. "Actually, I was going to thank you for last night."

But that wasn't all. After what he'd heard and her reticence to start things up between them again, he knew she was going to try to brush him off. Now that he knew she cared, he wasn't going to let her push him away.

"No need to thank me. Especially since I'm hoping we can have an encore tonight."

It stung that she checked the weather with a fleeting glance before answering. "I don't know if that's such a good idea."

He stepped close and brushed his lips against hers. "Just think about it. I'll find you. But right now, I have a few things I have to take care of."

She studied him for a moment. "All right."

He took the tiny victory. "See you tonight."

He left before she could say anything else. He'd all but seen the cogs in her head working. The snow hadn't quite let up yet, but it could at any moment. Ana seemed like the type who wouldn't sit around if things finally went her way. And why would she when it sounded as though it was life or death for someone she desperately cared about.

Still, they were after the same diamond—and so were a lot of other people. There were so many angles to consider…

He had a lot to think about.

Rhys departed without a fuss, which left Ana puzzling over how easy it had been to get him out of there. That was weird. He had practically run when she had been positive that she was going to have to convince him to leave. Still, she couldn't dwell on him. Not when Marco was losing patience. There had to be a way to get out of this place. Even if it was by dog sled, she was willing to consider it.

How much of a moron was she to waste her time in bed with Rhys when she should have been getting that diamond and figuring a way out?

Her stomach fluttered when she thought about the night before. They had woken several times in the night hungry for each other and had found some very satisfying ways of sating their rampant desire. It had been amazing, just as it had been before. Just as she knew it would be again.

She had been an idiot to let it happen.

Still, it had been damn good.

The wonderful, bone-deep relaxation she'd felt upon waking this morning had been blasted away with a single text from Marco.

The bastard had sent pictures of Eric sleeping. He'd taken them from the window — she could tell from the vantage point — but the threat was clear. And she wasn't going to take it lying down. He thought he could just waltz into her life, do whatever the hell he wanted and order her around? Ana had been planning retribution, but Marco was taking things too far now.

The terror and the anger mixed in her blood to create a potent combination that fueled her. Focused her mind.

Ana ordered room service. The objective being she wasn't going to leave the room until she had a plan she could pull off the instant she knew the snow was letting up. Then she'd have the diamond and be out of there before anyone caught on.

Bolstered by the idea, she took a quick shower and got dressed.

Housekeeping had been by while she'd been in the

bathroom and the result was miraculous, as though a team of magical elves had swept through the room. Everything was made up, fresh and new. The bed had been made, the flowers replaced—where they'd found fresh, snow-white orchids at this altitude, she'd never know—even her clothes had been put away. If only she had the same people working in her home.

Ana snickered at the thought. The money she had acquired from the various jobs over the years had definitely made life easier. She could afford help, but the trust that had to come before having someone in her home so regularly… that wasn't established easily. So for the most part, it was exclusively her and Eric.

She actually couldn't wait for it to be that way again. Ana was willing to do whatever it took to keep him happy, safe and shielded from the shit that the world had to offer. And she would keep it up as long as she could.

At least she had a few years yet to worry about him venturing even a little way out of her protective bubble.

More pressing concerns weighed on her mind right now.

Like the photo of Eric on her dresser.

Identical to the one that Marco had sent her, it was obviously a message from him. With a shaking hand, she picked it up and traced the image of his dark hair and plump cheeks. She would never let anything or anyone hurt him.

There had to be something she could do to before she went crazy. Or Marco refused to wait any longer. There was no telling what he would do once he reached the end of his fraying and already short tether.

An idea started to form in her mind. It wasn't ideal, but she and Rhys were both after the same thing. Maybe he would be willing to work together…

Then she would have to find a way of convincing him to let her have it. If he didn't… Well, she would have to figure that out if it came to it.

Obviously, Marco had a closer eye on things than she

realized. Her suite had lost the last illusion of safety. Ana shivered and hated that he could affect her from so far away.

She immediately ruled out looking for another room, there was no chance of that with the ball and the storm. She had no true friends there, and even if she did, she couldn't put them in danger.

That left Rhys.

She packed as her mind reeled with different ways she could approach Rhys without making it obvious what she was doing. He could protect himself and watch her back if she needed it, though putting him in danger wasn't something that appealed, he was more than capable of taking care of himself. He just wouldn't be thrilled that her reason for moving into his suite was the furthest thing from sex.

Or. She could tell him the truth and forgo the games to approach him honestly. The idea of telling him everything scared her almost more than what Marco was capable of. Frightening or not, it was worth a try.

She shoved all of her belongings into the bag and headed for the door then opening it in time to see Rhys lifting his hand to knock.

"Hey, I was just coming to…" His expression shuttered as he dragged her out of the room. "What's wrong?"

Ana thought she would have at least the trip up to this suite to settle her nerves. Caught off-guard, she grabbed his hand and started walking.

Rhys let her but said, "Ana? You're freaking me out."

"Someone was in my room while I was in the shower," she mumbled.

"What? Who?" Rhys slowed and turned to investigate.

She grabbed him again and determinedly pulled him along, wanting as much space between them and the suite as possible. "They're not there now. And I have no idea who it was."

"How do you know?" He tugged her back so that they

could walk side by side. "Never mind. You're staying with me."

Though she had been hoping he would say that, Ana wasn't sure if it was nerves or apprehension or even happiness at his offer that flipped her stomach.

Being together in such close quarters wasn't going to be easy.

She looked up at him and caught the concerned yet angry expression on his handsome face.

Or maybe it would be too easy.

Seeing Ana pale and obviously shaken had thrown him for a loop. There was no question of where she would be staying. The fact that she had her things packed and agreed so readily spoke volumes about her state of mind.

That worried him more than anything else. An adversary who was after him was one thing, but this was something entirely new. Not knowing who or what was after Ana was going to keep him awake and on edge until they were out of the way.

He had come by to see if she was up to hanging out. And by hanging out, he meant trying to persuade her to let him help. It was obvious what she was after. Knowing what he did about the diamond, whoever was forcing her to steal it wasn't doing it for the betterment of mankind. Maybe if he could get to them first and stop the pressure on Ana, she would be free to walk away.

Because he wasn't going to let either fall into the wrong hands.

Anyone who would coerce someone else into doing their bidding by harming someone else definitely fit the criteria for being exactly the wrong hands for the diamond to be in.

As much as he feared for her, the fact that they would be sharing a suite both excited and pleased him. At least now he could keep a close eye on her and help keep her from harm. Not to mention she might even be amenable to a repeat of the night before.

He shoved aside the voice of his selfish inner caveman and focused.

First he had to get her settled in his suite before she got over the shock and wanted to find another option.

Rhys didn't say a word as he led the way up to the penthouse, concerned that any little thing, no matter how tiny, would snap her out of it and she would change her mind.

It wasn't until he unlocked the door and stepped inside the penthouse that he released the breath he hadn't realized he'd been holding.

Giving her a miniscule smile, he waved her in. "Make yourself at home."

"Thanks."

The vacant look in her eyes wasn't doing anything to alleviate the sinking feeling he had inside, so he took her bag and ushered her into the living area. Sitting her down, Rhys made sure she was okay before he reached for the phone. "I'll call for some breakfast."

"Okay." She licked her lips and continued to stare at an unknown point in the distance.

It was then that he realized that she wasn't freaking out. She was thinking, very intently. If he guessed correctly, she was plotting. And why wouldn't she be? If anyone had upset him as badly as Ana had been, there would be a fair bit of plotting going on in his head, as well.

What he wanted was to get inside her mind to figure out what she was so furiously planning. Even more, he wanted details on what had happened. What had scared her so badly that she'd practically ran into his arms?

He made the call and went to the kitchen. Coffee? That might perk her up a little. A quick cup before the meal arrived wouldn't hurt.

By the time he brought back two steaming mugs, Ana had her phone out and was typing furiously on it.

He put her mug down in front of her then sat, watching and waiting patiently for her to finish.

Several long minutes later, she dropped the phone disgustedly onto the couch. It was only after raking her hands through her hair a few times and a deep and gusty sigh that she looked at him.

"Thanks again, Rhys."

"You don't have to thank me. I'm hardly going to leave you without help, am I?"

It was plain on her face that she thought he might have. Sure, things between them hadn't been smooth, but he liked to think he was a good guy. He would never leave her in danger if he could avoid it. And he had hoped that she knew that much about him as well.

"So you want to clue me in on what's going on?" Rhys could see that she was trying to piece something together in her head. He wasn't going to let her fabricate a story. Taking her hands, he tugged on them until she focused on him. "The truth."

He never expected that his demand would bring tears. His usually cool, confidant Ana turned to him. Her huge whiskey-colored eyes silently pleaded with him.

"Shit, Ana." He hauled her closer. "Take your time."

She clung to him and cried into his chest. Sobbed. Rhys had no idea what to do but smooth her hair and let her drench his shirt as she cried herself out. It was as unnerving as much as it heartened him that she would allow herself to be vulnerable in front of him.

"I'm sorry," Ana mumbled into his soaked pec. She tried to pull away, but he wouldn't let her go. She gave up struggling and tipped her head back to stare up at him. "Rhys, I need your help."

How could he say no?

He knew he couldn't let her get away with the diamond, but he'd do anything to help her out short of that. Anything to get the frightened, haunted expression off her face. To get the trust back in her eyes when she looked at him.

Gingerly, he turned her around to rest against him. "Tell me how."

Ana craned her head around to gaze up at him. "I need that diamond."

"You know I do, as well."

She turned to stare straight ahead. "I know."

Now was a good chance to get some information out of her. He jostled her a little until she twisted to meet his gaze again. "Maybe if you tell me why you need it?

He regretted the question immediately when her eyes filled again. Still, he needed to know what was going on if he was going to do anything about it.

She took a deep breath.

Was she really going to tell him everything?

Ana licked her lips. She'd already cried in front of him. There was no one she had done that in the presence of since she'd been a child. It was now or never. "You know how I retrieve things for hire? Well, I used to, as in past tense. After what happened with you...what I thought happened to you...I did a couple of jobs afterward, but then I quit. I just wanted a quiet life."

Rhys nodded understandingly. "So what prompted the return?"

Her stomach flipped. "In my job, I work with people. Some good. Some not so much. One decided that I was the only one who could get a diamond he desperately wanted, so he made sure I couldn't say no."

Again, another nod. Rhys seemed so interested in hearing what she had to say she felt bad that all she cared about was her interest in the diamond.

"What about you? What's your fascination with it?"

Rhys looked somewhat annoyed that she asked him, but answered, "I'm trying to keep it out of the wrong hands."

That struck her as odd. "Why this diamond in particular? Why are so many people after it? I didn't get time to do my research as I usually would, but it seems weird that so many would be after this one." Diamonds were abundant enough that this one in such high demand was definitely alarming.

Rhys sighed. "I wish you weren't after it, too."

"Well, I am, so can't you tell me what's so special about it?"

He turned her around to face him fully. "It's inscribed with a formula for a drug that's supposed to make the world sit up and take notice. More addictive and destructive than anything ever conceived of before."

Something like that in Marco's hands was terrifying. But she still needed it to keep Eric safe.

He could see that she hadn't been deterred. "I see I haven't convinced you to back off."

"I can't."

He peered into her eyes. "Why not? What has this guy got over you?"

Ana stared right back at him. "He's threatening my baby, Rhys."

Baby? Ana had a baby? Rhys' head threatened to explode. Of all the possibilities, it had never entered his mind that she could be doing this to protect her child.

Then the jealousy hit, tangled tightly with anger and betrayal. Whose baby? So much for the grieving-widow act. Had she waited even a month before jumping into bed with someone else? A week?

Then to have the bastard's baby?

Rhys fought the urge to push her off and kick the coffee table over. It felt as though she had punched into his gut and tore out his intestines.

He gripped her arm. "How could you have a kid and not tell me?"

Ana balked, but she defiantly met his gaze. "I don't know. How could you be alive and not tell me?"

"How does one have anything to do with the other?" He understood now, her desperation to get the diamond, but he felt so betrayed the inclination to help her vaporized.

"Rhys." She held him down when he tried to get up.

"Stop."

Stop what? Being angry that she had someone else's baby? Stop raging because that baby should have been his?

Was that why she was reluctant to get involved with him again?

He had been such an idiot thinking about a future for them when she already had done so with someone else, that this had all been a ploy to get him to help her.

Fuck.

His entire body turned numb as she got up and went to her bag. She retrieved something that looked like a piece of paper. On the way back, she picked up her phone and quickly accessed something on it.

The tension and apprehension tightened her pale face. Ana's hand trembled slightly when she handed him the phone.

On the screen was a chubby baby with big eyes and dark curls. The toothless grin was almost cute.

Rhys glared at Ana. Was he supposed to think he was adorable and be willing to do anything for them? "And?"

She chewed her bottom lip before she whispered, "His name is Eric Rhys Stone. He's yours."

She witnessed the world fall out from under his feet yet again. In the span of a few minutes she'd managed to do it twice. Ana almost felt guilty. But watching that self-righteous fury turn into guilt, then trepidation, then into fury again was incredible.

He turned his gaze to the phone once more, his jaw slack as he gaped at the photo. She held out the one that had been left on her dresser.

"This photo was left in my room when I was in the shower. It's the same one that Marco sent to me this morning. Its meaning is clear. He's getting impatient."

Rhys looked at her as if she had been addressing him in a foreign language. "What?" He took the print of Eric and stared at it blindly.

"Marco Valente, he's the one who's threatening Eric. He's wants the diamond and doesn't care how he gets it."

"Marco Valente is the one behind this?" Rhys still hadn't stopped examining the photos. "That psycho has our kid?"

The way he said *our kid* warmed her heart a little, but the ice-cold glare he gave her when he lifted his gaze obliterated the sensation.

"How could you let this happen?"

Ana snatched the phone back, but he wouldn't relinquish the photo. "I didn't let anything happen. He caught me off-guard. I wasn't about to risk anything happening to my baby so here I am. The job sounded easy enough. A simple snatch and run."

"*Our* baby." The way he said it held a bit of awe under the steel. "Who's taking care of him now?"

"A couple of friends."

He stared at her wide-eyed. "A couple of friends are guarding him against a killer?"

Did he think so little of her? "It's not what you think. They're...colleagues."

His eyes narrowed. "So cons are watching him."

And there it was. He looked down on her. Shoving aside the stab of hurt, she snarled, "Would you rather people who know how to protect him are watching him, or a bunch of women from a knitting circle? All you need to know is that I trust them."

Rhys glowered at her. The shock and overload of information mixed with the anger and all the other emotions rampaging through him grew clear on his face.

"I'm supposed to trust you? You couldn't even be bothered to tell me I had a son!" The glare her gave her could have frozen a volcano. "How do I even know he's mine? This could be some trick solely to get my help. For all I know, there isn't even a kid."

Ana lurched to her feet.

She should have known he wouldn't take it well. What man would? And even if he was willing to accept that he had a child, she had kept the fact from him. That and there was so much between them that it would be amazing if he did believe her in the first place.

Stomach cramping, Ana realized it had been a colossal mistake to tell him anything. How could she have miscalculated his reaction so badly? All that talk about wanting to get back together with her was just that—talk. When it came down to it, when she'd finally opened up to him with the facts, he was proving who he truly really was.

An asshole.

Why had she thought any differently?

She grabbed her bag and slung it over her shoulder, giving him a deadly glare as she did. "Just stay out of my way, Rhys."

There was a resounding door slam, and she was gone.

Shit.

Rhys stared at the door, completely blindsided, paralyzed and wholly stunned at what had happened. Within minutes, he had gone from trying to convince Ana he was the one for her, to finding out he had a son, to completely alienating his baby's mother.

That was one for the books. If anyone thought they could beat this, he'd like to see them try.

He stared at the photo again. How could the kid *not* be his? All he had to do was look at him and he could tell. How old would that make him? Rhys couldn't tell by studying the photo but he figured a year and a half would be about right. Had Ana known while they were in Positano?

Rhys doubted it. He wanted to believe that she would have told him if she had.

Raking his hands through his hair, he forced himself to breathe.

He'd left Ana alone and pregnant. No wonder she was so angry and hurt. Yet more sins to heap onto the mounting pile.

And now she was pissed at him and on the rampage. Rhys

hoped that it wouldn't lead her to do something stupid, but she was a mother desperate to save her baby and angry on top of it. There was no telling what she was going to do. What she was willing to do.

Jesus. He had a kid. A son.

He understood the desperation Ana felt to do whatever she needed to get the diamond. The urge to protect them both was like a tidal wave crashing into him and it drove out the need to do anything else.

What the hell was he going to do now?

His mission had been to get the diamond and keep it out of all the wrong hands, but it if meant saving his son... Rhys didn't even have to think about it. He'd do whatever it took to make sure his flesh and blood was safe.

His son.

Pride started to fill him now, pushing out the seething mess of other emotions. He and Ana had made a baby. Now that the idea had had a chance to settle, how could he not swagger a bit?

Getting up, he grabbed the photo and shoved it carefully into his pocket. Hopefully, Ana had cooled off somewhat. He had some groveling to do.

He caught up with her as she stomped her way toward the elevator. Ana didn't even spare him a glance when he flanked her. Instead, she viciously stabbed the button — probably not for the first time — and glared straight ahead.

"Ana." He tried putting a gentle hand on her shoulder.

She swiped it away as if he was no more than a bug. "I told you to stay out of my way. I'm getting that diamond, even if I have to go through you to get it."

He tried to close a hand over her shoulder again only to have her repeat the action. Rhys wasn't going to stop trying, however. "Ana, I'm sorry. It was just a huge shock." Easing himself between her and the elevator, Rhys tried to get her to look at him. "Give me a chance to try to help you."

She slashed her hand through to air. "Why, so you can accuse me of lying again? Or so you have help taking the diamond for yourself to keep it out of the hands of people like me?"

Were those tears? Dammit. "Ana, come back to the suite with me. We can figure all of this out."

"I should have known that you would react this way when you found out what I used to do. And I should have guessed that the last thing you were interested in right now was a child. Now you know I'm a criminal with a baby in tow." She glared at him, teeth bared and eyes glittering. "Why would you want me?"

"Because I love you."

Chapter Ten

The words blasted the venom from her. Did she dare trust him? Suspicion narrowed her eyes. "Yeah, right. What angle are you playing?"

"The 'I'm a moron and I want to make things right by you' angle?"

She studied him. Rhys seemed sincere. The pallor was gone and the hollow shock that had emptied his eyes had as well. Ana wanted to believe him, was willing to give him the chance, but, in the meantime, she would continue to work toward getting that diamond. No matter what he was trying to pull, she could use it to her advantage.

His suite and protection was a start.

Ana turned her gaze up at him. "I want a separate room. I know your suite has more than one bedroom."

He looked relieved that she was even considering staying with him and nodded. "Of course."

"I need my space."

"Done."

"You say anything that resembles an accusation of me lying about Eric or that because of my job I'm somehow beneath you and I'll kick your ass."

The hopeful look fled from his face. "I never thought that."

"What was that about a couple of cons watching the baby?"

He frowned. "That's what they are."

"They're my friends and I work with them, so what does that make me?"

From the expression on his face, it hadn't occurred to him

that she would take his comment that way. "I apologize. I was in shock. I didn't mean to imply that you're the same as them."

She sighed. "But I am. You have to get used to that. If you can't, then I guess we have nothing to say to each another."

His eyes glittered like shards of glass. "I think we do." Rhys fished in his pocket and pulled out the photo of Eric. "This little guy needs a father."

Ana cursed herself for having said anything. "We have been doing fine without you."

"Really? Because the way I see it, you're being coerced into thievery by a murderer who is using our son against you as leverage. That's not something regular mothers have to worry about."

"And what makes you think you'd be a great father? You've been dead his entire life!"

It was the wrong thing to say.

Rhys grabbed her arm and dragged her back to the penthouse. The walls shuddered from the force of the door slam.

He spun her around and pressed her flat against the door. "I've apologized for that, several times over, I've given you my reasons. If you throw it in my face again—"

Ana shoved him, knowing full well that he was completely incensed and a simple move like that could turn this into another brawl. Not that she was afraid. She could use a good fight to release some tension.

She jammed her clenched hands into his shoulders, knocking him back half a step. "You'll what?"

He growled something incomprehensible as he crashed his mouth into hers. Ana hadn't known what to expect, but this definitely wasn't it.

It was infinitely better than another argument.

The hard, biting, angry kiss deepened as he navigated them through the suite. He tangled his hands in her hair, holding her head in place as he plundered her mouth. Ana was only too happy to let him. Each stroke of his tongue fanned the flames burning inside her. From the moment she'd seen him again, they were there, as embers ready to ignite. All it took was Rhys, his touch, a look from him, a smile, for them to burst into an inferno once more.

They bumped up against something, but neither of them was bothered enough to stop. Instead, he used it to his advantage and pressed her into it as he tore at her clothes, ripping them away so he could feel her skin.

Ana let him drag her clothes off before attacking his. Rhys pushed her back, laying her down on…felt? It wasn't until Rhys swept his arm over her head that she heard the clack of the balls and realized she was on a massive pool table.

She didn't get much chance to think any more than that before Rhys pushed himself into her. No preliminaries, no finesse, only raw need to be inside her. To claim her.

Exultant in his possession, Ana gripped him to her, meeting his almost savage thrusts with ones of her own.

So much pleasure. Even though the anger was evident, she knew he wouldn't hurt her. The emotions raging through him added an edge to the always-stellar sex. Ana relished it, giving as much as she received.

Her orgasm caught her off guard. Convulsing under him, she screamed into his shoulder as the pleasure crashed over her.

Rhys plunged into her almost mindlessly, seeking his own release. Gripping her hips, he roughly pushed into her again and again. But clearly just his pleasure wasn't enough for him. Rhys held her gaze, seeming to almost dare her to come again. How could she not when he had drawn out her last orgasm and was steadily building her up to another, even more devastating one?

His face blurred as he grew impossibly bigger and harder inside her a scarce moment before she exploded again. Ana fought not to close her eyes in the wake of the waves of pleasure so she could see his face contort almost painfully as he pulsed inside her, coming with a shout.

Rhys moved his hips reflexively, drawing out the sparks

of pleasure until he was too spent to move.

For a long moment, they lay entwined on the pool table. Ana was sure he was as stunned as she was by how fast and primal it had been. She had been swept up in the hurricane and now that the storm had passed, uncertainty was starting to set in.

What the hell was she thinking?

As usual, when it came to him, she had let her hormones get the best of her. Why couldn't she think straight when Rhys was involved?

But though she tried to get up, he didn't move. In fact, she could feel his erection coming back to life inside her.

"Rhys."

"Ana," he grumbled her name into her neck as he thrust experimentally. He had half a mind to keep her under him for the rest of their lives. It was the one place they didn't have any problems. Any arguments. Only heat, pleasure, passion.

It was perfection.

They had so much to sort out. It could all wait.

He pushed into her firmly and was rewarded with a gasp. Rhys pulled back and did it again and again. Ana gazed up at him with the look she used to give him when they made love. It was something he wanted from her — in and out of bed.

Now that he knew they had a child together…

Rhys was going to do whatever it took to convince her that they could make things work. Even if it meant bending her over every surface he could find and turning her mind to mush with sex.

An endeavor he'd gladly throw himself into if he needed to.

Ana's sleepy responses to him grew bolder. He loved knowing that he could drain all the strength from her and bring her to life under him once more. Watching the transformation was a wonder each time. It was in her eyes

116

mostly. While her body would burn under him, it was the change in her eyes that captivated him. The change in color, how they darkened just before she climaxed, the way they seemed to see everything about him and nothing at all at the same time fascinated him.

Rhys climbed onto the table now, folding her under him until her knees hooked over his shoulders. It allowed him deeper penetration and full view of her beautiful face as he plunged into her. On the second thrust, Ana squealed and clawed at his shoulders, letting him know he had hit the spot that drove her crazy. Biting her lush bottom lip, she held his gaze, something she knew he loved, pushing up and meeting his thrusts. The depth of penetration caught his breath, yet it wasn't enough. He wanted more. Rhys wanted her screaming from the pleasure only he could give her.

He sank into her — his thrusts quicker, harder — until he pushed her over the edge once more with his name on her lips.

Definitely something he'd never tire of.

He eased back a bit so she could unfurl herself. Rhys thrust himself deep once more, aligning their bodies so that as much skin would touch as possible as they lay entangled on the table.

Ana wound herself around him, as if she couldn't stand anything separating them. She urged him deeper, harder, faster, until he couldn't hold himself back any longer.

Still he fought against the inevitable. Rhys reveled in the pleasure, in the fact that he gave the same to her. He wanted it to last. He wanted to make her feel like this forever. He groaned into her neck as the pleasure boiled over in his pelvis and he shot into her, slowly thrusting while the cascade of sensation threatened to drown him.

Trembling from the aftershocks, he gazed down at Ana who stared up at him blindly, still dazed from her orgasm.

Rhys loved her. Everything about her, no matter how maddening or infuriating she was, he loved her.

He withdrew and pulled her up with him then hopped off the table. Rhys easily picked up her pliant form and headed to the magnificent master bathroom. Turning on the water, he waited until he was sure of the temperature before he slipped her in one end. He darted from the room to retrieve a bottle of champagne that had been sitting in the chiller since he'd arrived. Minutes later, he had two glasses poured and sank into the tub behind her. It was heaven to have Ana in his arms and the hot water easing the aches away.

Ana hadn't said a word. She did, however, stretch out as she reached for a glass. Rhys snagged it first and handed it to her then retrieved his own. He certainly wasn't going to be the one to ruin the serenity of the moment.

With a sigh, he sipped his drink and settled back.

"You know we can't spend all our time naked. We eventually have to get dressed and face reality."

"Eventually." As long as they were snowed in, he was certainly willing to endeavor to spend as much time as possible without clothing. Then again, there was the issue of the monster holding his son.

"I don't want you to get mad, or get out, or get indignant now." He felt her tense at his words. "But can you fill me in on…everything?"

There was a long pause, an equally long sip from her glass. She slowly began to relax. "How far back do you want me to go?"

He cleared his throat. "From the explosion." She tensed and there was a slight tremor in her taut figure. "If it bothers you…"

"I'm fine." Though, from the strain in her voice, he would have thought otherwise.

Ana was glad her back was to him. It made it easier for her to tell her side of things.

"I told you how I was devastated by losing you. The word doesn't even describe what I went through." Ana still couldn't begin to explain the devastation that she had endured thinking that he had died. All at once she had felt as though she had died with him, but also rage and sorrow. Then at times numb before it gave way to pain so great it was as if she was going to explode from the force of it.

Ana took a stuttering breath. "I went in...afterward... to see for myself where you died. It was as if I needed to prove that you were gone." The destruction was total, as if everything had been touched by an evil scourge intent on wiping the premises off the face of the earth. All she could remember seeing were scorched remnants of wall. Pieces of what could have been furnishing. Each step she'd taken into the wreckage had caused a larger part of her heart to shatter until she had scarcely been able to breathe.

Remembering made her heart clutched even now. The memories brought back the emotions as real and raw now as they had been at the time.

"I saw what I was told was your body in the morgue. I think that's when it truly hit me that you were gone. I can't really remember much else about that time. I had sunk into a depression so deep I could hardly eat or sleep. Cried until I was sick." She laughed ruefully. "It was a few months before I realized that the sickness was due to something else entirely."

His arms tightened around her, but he stayed silent, waiting for her to continue.

"I had thrown myself into work in the hopes of clearing my head and moving on with my life, before I realized I was pregnant."

Rhys ran his free hand up and down her arm soothingly.

It was surprisingly easy to tell him. Ana supposed that she had been wanting to tell him everything the entire time. The words just tumbled out.

Ana cringed as she remembered the risks she had taken not only with her own life but the little spark of one that had been growing inside her.

The first assignment she had taken straight afterward had

led her to scale the outside of a skyscraper in Abu Dhabi in the quest of a paltry ruby. The one after that she'd been so close to being caught she had been grazed by a bullet from a pursuing guard. On the next, she had forsaken the easier path and again chose to nearly kill herself to retrieve an antique jeweled dagger.

They were a few in a long line of stupid risks she'd taken. It took Ana some time to realize that she had been looking for an adrenaline rush out of desperation to make herself feel alive again.

None of it had worked, however.

Then came the morning when she had to admit to herself that the shakiness, the queasiness, how wrong she felt wasn't purely grief. Ana remembered how her hand had trembled when she'd looked at the test. How incredibly happy and terrified when the clear result had stared her in the face.

The shaking hadn't subsided even after taking six different tests. It might have gotten worse when the diagnosis had been confirmed by a doctor.

"Once I figured out I was pregnant, I quit. There was no question about my decision. No doubt. No hesitation. I wanted peace and quiet and safety for my baby, so I took the money I had and moved to a little village here in France. I bought a secluded old millhouse and fixed it up. I told no one where I was except for a trusted few. I thought it was safe, that no one would find us, because no one would come looking. As far as anyone in the town was concerned, I was a single mother searching for a simple life for her and her baby."

He turned her slightly so he could meet her gaze. "If I had known...I never would have left you."

She managed a half-smile. "That's easy to say now."

Rhys glowered. "You think I would have willingly left you or our baby? I did what I thought was right at the time. I needed to keep you safe while I dealt with all this. Instead, I managed to do the complete opposite. I abandoned you when you needed me most." He sighed. Rehashing the same thing yet again wasn't going to help anything. They both knew that. "When did Valente show up?"

Bile rose in her throat at the name. "A few days ago. Before that, we'd done a few jobs together. There was always something about him that rubbed me the wrong way. He was too…everything. No one got on with him. Eventually, he was phased out and no longer called on for jobs. No one thought any more about him."

"He laid low until now."

"You seem to know about him." Ana cocked her head so she could get a better read of Rhys. "Had you run into him before?"

"I've heard of him. Never had the pleasure of dealing with him personally." The look on his face had her thinking that he would relish confronting him right at that moment.

"So far he hasn't done more than make it clear that he's watching the house and is willing to do whatever it takes to get the diamond. Now that I know why, it all makes sense."

"I'm going to twist his head off."

Ana believed the growl from the man behind her.

There was a long silence.

"Can you tell me about…Eric? Was it hard…having him?"

She let out a gusty laugh. "It wasn't a picnic. I was sick and so tired in the beginning. Then I was in labor about twenty hours."

"Alone?" he choked the word out.

"I had a couple of friends with me. The ones watching him now, actually." She glanced at him. "They really would give up their lives for him. They're his family."

"*I'm* his family," the words came out as if they were gravel scraping up his throat as he turned her to face him. "You named him for me…and I knew nothing about him."

Pity actually wormed its way into her heart, stopping her from reminding him it was his fault he was ignorant of her son's existence.

"He's a happy little boy. Does have his sulks, though.

Especially when he doesn't get his way." She peeked over her shoulder at him. "I guess he's just like his daddy in that sense."

Rhys scowled at her, though it quickly turned back into curiosity and awe. "He's like me?"

"Yes, he is. He looks like you, too. Even gets the same pout going," she teased.

"I don't pout."

"What do you think you're doing right now?"

He splashed her. Ana laughed and retaliated. The weight she had been carrying was gone. At least as far as telling Rhys about things was concerned. Now all there was to do was save her baby and make sure the man threatening him never did the same to anyone ever again.

Ana downed the rest of her glass and set it aside. "I'm going to take Marco out." She challenged him with a glare. "Are you going to help?"

Rhys nodded curtly. "Whatever it takes."

She smiled. "Then we have to come up with a plan."

Smiling in response, he jostled her. "I've always wondered how a criminal's mind works."

Chapter Eleven

Rhys watched Ana, utterly fascinated. The way she pursed her lips when she was in deep thought, how she tangled her fingers in the ends of her hair. Even the glassy faraway look in her eyes as she pondered captivated him.

He wound a lock of her hair around his finger as she talked. They had gotten out of the bath and into bed, where they stayed naked and entwined as if it was something they did all the time.

The tension between them had shifted almost palpably. Spending the morning with her was flirty and almost fun. At least it would have been if circumstances were different.

Though he definitely got an insight into the inner workings of her mind.

Ana's brain worked at dizzying speeds. Yet she could only plan so far thanks to the weather.

What he enjoyed the most, however, was being a part of it all. Kicking ideas around and helping her formulate something that could work. She was more skilled then he had imagined. Rhys knew that she had the soul of an artist, but he had no clue that she was also gifted with technology and her logic with devices was noteworthy. If she had been interested, he would have put her up for a job with the agency he was with.

At any rate, he had no plans to go back to work after this. He wanted to hide her away from the world. To simply be the two — no — the three of them.

He was done with that life. Had been for the past couple of years. When he had met Ana he knew that what he had once called his life was over. He just needed to get closure on Greg Rutherford's death. His partner would be avenged.

It had been a long chain of events that Rhys never would have thought would lead him to where he was now. Back with Ana. Working with her. Finding out he was a father. That still was surreal. He understood that he had a son. Rhys even looked forward to meeting him, but until he did it probably wouldn't sink in properly.

He took out the photo again and studied it.

And cold dread seeped into his veins. What the hell did he know about being a dad? His own hadn't been the loving type. Their contentious relationship had been the reason he'd left home straight out of high school and had never looked back.

Could he even *be* a father?

Rhys swallowed the knot of apprehension. He wouldn't let his son think of him as an asshole or a failure as a parent.

It didn't stop him from getting nauseated at the thought of turning out like his own dad.

"Hey. You just turned a weird shade of green. Are you okay? Have you changed your mind about working with a thief?" She said it jokingly, but it was clear on her face that Ana was serious about his answer.

"Not at all." Rhys forced a smile. "I'm a little worried about whether my skills will match up with yours."

She searched his eyes but thankfully didn't push it. "You'll do fine, I'm sure. It's nothing you haven't done before."

Not raising someone, he hadn't.

He willed his muscles to unbunch. One thing at a time. He had to ensure Eric's safety before he needed to worry about raising him.

Until it was time to actually get the diamond, Rhys was totally and completely committed to the role he was to play. The doting lover of a countess in a luxury hotel.

As far as characters he'd had to portray, this one was, and always would be, his favorite.

"So are you going to tell me how you managed to get the penthouse at the Totally Five Star Hotel in Chamonix for the Winter Ball?"

He chuckled. "Like you, I've amassed some cash over the years. I'm more than comfortable now with the cover identity of a wealthy socialite looking to spend a little and enjoy myself very much at the party of the year."

She took a moment to consider that before asking, "And how did you get talking to Christine?"

Was that a tinge of jealousy in her voice?

He hid the smile. "The same way you did, I should think. She was a direct line of information to the diamond."

Another pause. Ana rolled, sliding her creamy skin against his to rest on his stomach. A sight he could get used to. "And just how did you get information out of her?"

Definitely jealousy.

Rhys found he liked Ana getting territorial about him. Not that she needed to be. He kissed her again. "I only talked to her. I promise you. The truth is, there hasn't been anyone else since you."

Her eyes rounded slightly.

"As I told you, I was coming back to you. In my mind, there was never a moment there wasn't an 'us'." Rhys' stomach roiled when it occurred to him why she could possibly assume that he was with someone else. "Was there…anyone else for you?"

She shook her head and held his gaze steadily, her eyes clear. "No. Never."

Hauling her up for a kiss, Rhys vaguely wondered if he was dreaming. Maybe all this was just a mirage. Maybe he was in a hospital bed somewhere and this was a delusion. To finally be back in the arms of the woman of his dreams, have a son…it was too good. He'd never been this content. Not even back in Positano.

The dread was there. That this was going to fall apart. Because it would. It always had. Nothing good in his life had lasted.

Rhys sincerely wished that this would. That what he had with Ana would last and grow into something concrete. He wrapped his arms around her and held her close, almost wanting to convey his wish without words. He wasn't too proud to admit that it pleased him when she did the same.

It was so easy to believe in that moment that, together, they could take on the world.

Ana stretched. "We should probably make an appearance, to keep up the pretense that we're a couple."

He chuckled. "So it's all a sham, is it?"

"You know what I meant." She sighed and shimmied against him, trying to slip away.

If it was up to him they would never leave the room. Rhys had to remind himself that there was someone else he had to consider now. And he would do whatever it took to keep him safe.

So he let her slide off the bed and smiled as she padded naked out of the room in search of her bag. That was another thing he loved about her. She was totally unashamed of her body. Not that she had any need to be. Ana was perfection.

"I'm getting in the shower," she called from the hall. "You're welcome to join me."

As much as he wanted to, he knew it was too much temptation and if she wanted to make it out sometime today he had to stay out. "I'll take one in the en suite."

Her lilting laughter followed her as she disappeared into the bathroom and shut the door.

Rhys grumbled to himself willing his cock not to react to the sound and the mental image of Ana naked and wet.

Instead of following her into the other room like his body ached to do, he stalked into the joining bathroom. Turning on the shower, he made sure that it was cold enough to blast any thoughts of dragging Ana back into bed with him. Hopefully, it would help him get his head in gear.

He stepped under the stream of water, but the chill didn't bother him as much as he'd hoped it would. Rhys removed the rest of the heat with a flick of his wrist.

When Ana had said Marco Valente was the one who had threatened their baby, rage had consumed him. Why was it whenever something shit happened in his life that asshole was the one at the heart of it?

After Rutherford had died in the explosion, it had taken him a couple of months to track down the perpetrator. Rhys wasn't going to rest until he found out who had done it and why. And most definitely not until he got retribution.

What struck him as odd was that even when he'd thought Ana was safely out of the picture, Marco was a suspiciously convenient link between them.

Was it really a coincidence that Ana had worked with Marco previously and all of a sudden she was there to steal a diamond Rhys himself was after?

The possibility that he was being masterfully played was very real. Would Ana really do that to him? He didn't think that she was capable of something so horrible. Then again, up until recently, he never imagined she could be a thief, either.

The niggling idea that she was in league with the man who had killed Rutherford wouldn't completely die, however. He blamed the world he'd lived in his entire adult life for the nagging suspicion. There, lies and manipulations were a regular thing.

But was he still neck-deep in it?

Despite his gut telling him that he could trust Ana with his life, the irritating little voice in his head nagged him to slow down and think with something other than his dick.

Which still hadn't responded to the cold water so there was little chance of it paying any mind to his head.

Rhys had to protect himself in case he was being played.

There was a twinge of disappointment that Rhys hadn't followed her in. There was also a vague notion in the back of her mind to turn around and join him, but she thought better of it. While it felt great to be honest with Rhys, not to mention to connect with him again mentally and physically, they couldn't spend all their time together, even though it would be wonderful to do so.

With a smile, she stepped into the spray of water and let it sluice over her. The past couple of days had been a whirlwind of emotion. Ana knew things between them were far from settled, but they had come a long way from where they'd been when they'd first seen each other in the ballroom.

Knowing what she did about him, she was torn about whether or not everything he'd said was true.

He was hiding something from her. She could tell earlier that something had crossed his mind and it had upset him. It would take some time to get to the bottom of that. Having never worked with him before, what worried her was Rhys wouldn't be able to hold up his end of the plan. Whether it was skill-related or a moral dilemma didn't matter, if he didn't manage to keep it together to see things through she would never be able to forgive him.

Maybe it would be better to deal with things separately? She should come up with a failsafe, just in case.

As much as she hated imagining him letting her down, it was a possibility. Or worse, what if he got hurt and was incapacitated? She could barely stand to think about it. Ana knew her feelings for him were stronger than ever. If there were something she could do to keep him safe, wasn't it her duty to do it?

Knowing full well she was being a hypocrite, she braced herself for the conversation she was about to start.

Ana hurried through her routine, got out and dressed in a simple outfit of black trousers and a loose-fitting sweater. She dried her hair enough to twist it into a bun and slicked on a little gloss and was ready to go.

What she had to say to Rhys didn't require a lot of primping.

Her stomach twisted into knots as she walked into the en suite. "Rhys?"

"Decided to join me?" He stuck his head out of the glass enclosure with a grin. It dimmed a little when he saw she was dressed. They then darkened further when he focused on the serious expression on her face.

Rhys immediately twisted off the shower and stepped out. "What's wrong? Has something happened to Eric?"

She shook her head, but looked at a spot over his shoulder. "No. He's fine as far as I know. I came up with another idea."

Rhys crossed his arms and stared her down eyebrows creased together, seeming totally indifferent of his nude state. "What's going on?"

Ana's brain skipped a gear when she looked at him. There was no way she could stop looking. He was fit, wet — and fit — and scarred. The way the water gleamed on his skin...

She grabbed a towel and thrust it at him, refusing to say anything until he wrapped it around his lean hips before trying again.

"People will find it strange, won't they, seeing us together when we've only just met."

His eyebrows lowered even further. "So? People meet at hotels and fall into each other's beds all the time. Besides, I already laid the groundwork for us having a past with Cabral and the security guard."

What else could she say? Ana tried it from another angle. "Christine has a thing for you. You need to exploit that somehow. She won't be as cooperative if she sees us as a couple."

"That may be true." He stepped closer and clearly tried to use his size to intimidate her. "But that's not all there is to it."

She shuffled back. "I'm trying to cover all the angles. The better prepared we are the easier this will be."

Rhys continued to study her but then slowly started to nod. "All right. So you want to appear separately now."

"It's probably best to play it by ear for a little bit." She tore her gaze up from his pecs to meet his gaze. "What do you think?"

"You don't want to know what I think." He shrugged and gave her an indolent look. "We'll play it your way. For now."

That sounded ominous. But she would take it.

"Okay." Ana peered into his eyes. "You're angry."

"Because you're changing things up on me for some reason." He glared at her. "I want to know why."

"This is how I work. I find that adapting to changing circumstances had kept me from getting caught. If you don't like that—"

"That's not it. You're hiding something."

Ana met his gaze, daring him to lie again. "And you're not?"

He grumbled something as he stalked from the room. Ana followed to find him tugging clothes on.

"So what's wrong? You've decided you can't work with a criminal? Does it offend you working with someone so beneath you?"

He deftly buttoned his shirt. "That's bullshit and you know it. If who you are bothered me, I would have bolted the moment I found out."

"You could be staying because of Eric." She narrowed her eyes. "Unless you've decided I'm lying about him."

Rhys raked a hand through his hair, whipping the remaining water away. The thought had occurred to him. As had so many others. There was so much between them that was unknown or questionable that he wasn't sure what to believe.

All he knew was that she was an enigma that he had incredible sex with. Everything else could very well be a lie.

His stomach dropped when she paled.

"You don't believe me." He tried to put a hand on her arm, but she brushed it away. "No. Don't."

The pain in her eyes gutted him but he needed to be honest with her. "I want to believe you. And I do. To a point." He sighed. "It's just all so surreal and so fast. It won't fully sink in until I see him for myself, I guess. And then what? I had a shitty childhood. What if I'm a shit dad, too?"

From the confusion and realization that was on her face it had never occurred to her that he had been considering these things. That he had any doubts to his ability to be a father.

She swallowed and looked up at him. "I've been concerned, too. I wasn't lying when I said I want to cover all the angles. But I've never worked with you before. So if we split up and stick to what we do best, things might work out better. And then there's the part of me that wants to keep you safe…"

Rhys relaxed a little. Her worries were valid. They made sense. This was a job that was too important for her to let it fall apart.

They were both so guarded. So jaded. It stung to think that she didn't trust him fully, but could he blame her? He had the same apprehensions.

Pulling her in for a hug, he wanted to disappear from the world with her and get to know his son.

Ana wriggled in his arms and he immediately let go. Had she changed her mind about him?

But she was fiddling with something in her pocket. Ana fished out her phone. A few quick taps of the screen and there was a ring tone. It barely rang twice before a handsome man appeared on the screen. There went the hope of her friend being an ugly, fat, balding man. He could still hope for him being short, at least.

"Ana? What's wrong?" Concern etched itself into his face. He glanced to Ana's side and noticed Rhys. His expression morphed into angry understanding as he snorted. "Needs proof, does he?"

Ana sighed. "I just needed to see Eric, Javi."

"Very well." He looked at Rhys again. "We will have to talk, you and I."

Ana wasn't kidding about the protectiveness of her friend. Rhys gave him a slight nod. "We will."

Javier didn't bother with a reply. He walked through the house giving Rhys a brief glimpse into Ana's home. It looked cozy. Feminine. He caught glimpses of décor from all over the world. Pretty much what he'd expected of her.

Then he approached a little room. Rhys could hear another voice, a woman this time, speaking softly. Javier turned the camera to show a slight woman with tumbling blonde curls tickling a baby on his belly on the floor in the middle of a toy explosion.

Eric chortled with delight, before flipping over and crawling to retrieve a toy. With it in his hand, he pushed himself to his feet and unsteadily tottered his way back to proudly present it to her.

"Hey, Sara." Ana smiled at her friend. "How are things going?"

"Everything's fine here. I hear you can't say the same on your end." Her blue-green gaze flitted to Rhys. She considered him a moment ultimately deciding he wasn't worth addressing. Her attention returning to Ana, she asked, "When do you think you'll be back?"

"I'm hoping a day or two tops, but there's no telling with the weather." Ana paused to smile at her baby as he babbled away. "Has Javier been behaving himself?"

"I'm being a gentleman, which is more than I could say for your friend here," said Javier behind the camera. "She's a harpy who doesn't think I know how to take care of a child."

"He's sore because Eric loves his Aunty Sara better than that mean old Javier, don't you, sweetheart?" She tickled the little boy again.

Rhys's heart clutched. He might not have been an expert on children, but he could see that Eric was healthy and happy. And that he looked almost exactly like him. It was striking even through the camera. The dark hair and eyes. Eric even had his nose. He might as well have been his clone.

"Give him a kiss for me, Sara. I've got to go. Love to you both."

The woman on the screen nodded. "See you soon."

It took him a moment to get what he had seen into his head. "You didn't have to do that."

"I figured it was the one way to resolve one of the issues between us." She put the phone back in her pocket.

"Your friends don't like me." Neither had seemed particularly receptive to him. Rhys could only imagine what they thought of what he had done, no matter what the motivation.

"They don't know you. All they know is you faked your death and have been miraculously resurrected. Once they get to know you, they'll like you. And vice versa."

Ana knew little more than that but she was opening up to him. It gave him some hope that at the end of this there was going to be something concrete waiting.

If there wasn't going to be a relationship with Ana, at least he still had his son.

"Are you okay?"

Rhys nodded. "Fine. Thank you, for that. For having him."

She gave him a small smile. "There was no question of that. I loved him the moment I found out I was expecting."

And he hadn't been there for any of it. The fact crushed him. He had missed the wonder of finding out Ana was pregnant, the early days, watching her body change and grow, Eric's birth, sleepless nights... He'd missed out on so much that he would never get to experience.

He shoved the guilt and self-recrimination aside, clearing his mind to keep it on task. "So you want us to stick to what we know, huh?"

Ana nodded slowly. "Talk to Christine. Find out everything you can about the diamond, the security. Anything and everything we can use. I'll take another look around and see what I can figure out."

Nodding, he made a mental list of everything he could find out. "Right. We'll meet back here...?"

"Tonight." She paused and he knew he wasn't going to like what she was going to say. "I want to see if I can figure out who's working for Marco, as well."

"Ana..."

She waved his concern away. "You have enough to worry about with Christine. If you want something else to do, you can try to weed out the idiot who attacked me last night. They might even be the same person as the one working for Marco."

He got the impression she was trying to keep him out of the way. But why?

She stared at him. "I can practically see your brain working, you know."

Rhys rolled his eyes. "So you're trying to keep me out of the way, but the question is why. Is it because you don't trust me to hold my own, or because you want to do stuff that you don't want me to see?"

It was as if the air around her froze. "What is it about me that screams 'do not trust'?"

Rhys closed his hands over her shoulders. "It's not you. You have to admit that the world we've lived in doesn't exactly give you gleaming expectations of human nature. I don't mean to distrust you. It's...hard for me. I pictured you as someone else for so long...to find out that you're someone completely different changed things in my head..."

Her pointed look triggered the realization that it was the same for her.

They were in the same boat.

"I'm such an idiot." He dragged her into the cage of his arms. "I'm sorry. We both have a lot of baggage and our relationship hasn't exactly been conventional. I need to remember that."

"Yeah, you do." She hesitantly hugged him back. "But I honestly think that until we can get over...all this...we should split up and approach it in our own way."

He nodded. "Right. Just be careful, okay?

She squeezed him tightly. "You, too."

Chapter Twelve

Ana walked into the biggest bar in the hotel. Since the storm had hit, it had unsurprisingly become one of the major congregating places for hotel patrons to spend their time. If there was news to be had, she was more than likely going to hear it here first. Alcohol made the whole process easier and since it was getting on in the day, there were bound to be more than a few people who would relax themselves right into her hands.

She ordered a drink, purely for ornamental purposes, and scanned the room. Ana had hoped to see Cabral around. He'd rubbed her the wrong way from the beginning and it dawned on her that he might be after the diamond too. It just seemed too easy. He was up to something, however. Then again, who wasn't? But Ana wanted to rule him out as a competitor.

"Ana, darling!" Ciara waved at her from a table against the window.

Plastering a smile on her face, Ana walked over and took the seat her friend fluttered her fingers at.

"It's been deadly dull in here. Please tell me you have something interesting to share."

Ana shrugged. "Sorry. It seems being trapped in a hotel isn't as fun as you'd think."

"You're telling me." Ciara pouted and took a sip of her cocktail.

Following her lead, Ana sampled her own drink. "Esteban not keeping you entertained?"

"The man has the attention span of a kitten. Always flitting off here and there."

That was information Ana filed away. The person who had attacked her had been a man. She couldn't say more than that, however. In the darkness, she hadn't been able to make out any features. He hadn't made a noise besides the groan when she'd hit him, so identifying him by voice would be next to impossible. Could it be Esteban? Possibly.

"I'm sorry to hear that."

"I hope your man is better at keeping you occupied."

"He's hardly my man." Ana stared at the snow whirling around outside for a long while before turning her gaze back.

"He certainly wants to be." She winked. "I can tell these things, you know."

"What else can you tell me about him?" This would be interesting.

"He's a good lover. Dedicated. You can tell that from his hands."

"Can you?" She knew both of those for a fact and, while his hands had helped her form that opinion, Ana wasn't about to elaborate.

Ciara nodded. "You can tell he really cares about you just looking at his eyes. The way they watch you like you're the only thing that matters in the world to him."

Ana's pulse fluttered a little. "I'm sure he's just curious."

"What I see isn't curiosity — it's covetousness. He wants you. I hope you make him work for it."

"I'm sure I will," Ana said into her glass as she took another sip. "Have you seen Mr. Cabral around?"

Ciara pouted her lips in a display of her disappointment. "Oh, darling, no. You want nothing to do with him."

No, she didn't, but she needed to find out where he'd been when she had been attacked.

"I was only wondering because he seems to find himself in the same places I do at the strangest moments. If I know where he is, I can avoid him that much easier."

"I see…" Ciara shrugged. "I couldn't tell you. The man is slipperier than an eel and about as appetizing." She shuddered dramatically.

Ana nodded in agreement. "I know what you mean."

"So where is your man? I assumed you spent the night together."

Ciara hadn't even tried to hide that attempt at mining gossip. Ana sighed. "Nothing quite that interesting happened. I told you I had a headache and arguing with that man wasn't going to help matters."

"Then you should have made sure you did something other than argue." Ciara sniffed as she swirled the remainder of her drink in the glass. It was obviously on her mind to order another. "We should get a bite to eat."

Might as well. Ana waved a waiter over. She was interested in what Ciara could tell her about Esteban.

"My life is so boring. I want to hear all about what you've been doing the past few years."

Ciara seemed barely able to contain herself as they ordered. When the waiter walked away, she bounced in her seat.

"Tell me about your Esteban. You two seem to have something real."

Her grin grew. "It does seem like the real thing, doesn't it?"

Ana sat back and let her talk.

"He's got more money than he could spend in four lifetimes, impeccable pedigree, and is so worldly and sweet. I wish he was a bit more attentive. As I said, he has a very short attention span. I suppose that comes with his age, though."

"How old is he?" Ana asked benignly. She figured he was young, but for that to be a factor it would have to be a big age gap.

"He's twenty-two."

Ana might not have known Ciara's age, but she knew there had to be nearly a decade difference between them. "That's not insurmountable."

"It isn't. But we're hardly thinking long term. At least not right now." She blushed a little when she looked at Ana. "I can see it happening, however."

The hope was that Esteban was true. She'd hate to see her friend hurt because of a lying jerk. "Where did you two meet?"

"A party. Two months ago."

The doubt swooped back into her gut. He would have known what was being exhibited at the Winter Ball at that point. A couple months of planning would be sufficient for an experienced thief, or would seem enough for one that was new and cocky.

"It was a whirlwind romance."

"Very much so." Ciara sighed happily as she gripped Ana's hand. "I wish you had the same in your life."

Fighting to keep her face neutral, Ana nodded. She didn't trust her voice just then. What she had with Rhys went far deeper than whatever Ciara thought she and Esteban had. And on top of it all, they had a child together. While they were still working to rebuild their relationship, she trusted Rhys enough to do whatever was in his power to protect her and their son.

To take it to the level Ciara thought she and Esteban were at, it would require a lot more time and conversation.

They both knew that, at least physically, they were good together. But like Rhys had said, the lives they'd led hadn't exactly been the best foundation when trying to form a committed relationship with anyone.

It wasn't a good foundation for anything, really.

She'd gotten into the life young, fresh out of college. Ana couldn't even remember the specifics of it. She'd been low on cash and a friend had introduced her to some people. She'd been recruited and the next thing she knew, it had been her life. And it had been a damn good one. The thrill and the travel. Rhys thought he'd had a bad childhood, but she would wager that her own would give him a run for his money. Before Eric had come along, she'd never really wanted to put down roots anywhere. Before Rhys, Ana hadn't considered settling down with anyone, either. It amused her that he had been the one to change her mind on both.

"I'm sorry. I didn't mean to upset you." Ciara gave her an apologetic and pitying look as the waiter returned with their orders.

In front of Ciara, the waiter placed a generous slice of a decadent chocolate torte and another mimosa, while Ana was given a large cinnamon bun slathered with a sinful amount of icing.

She picked at the sticky treat while Ciara took a fork full of hers, and groaned with delight. Ana's reaction was much the same. As far as cinnamon buns went, this one was perfect.

Ana was happy to let her think that Ciara had made her uncomfortable. "Where's Esteban from?"

"Heaven." Ciara giggled. "The things that man can do to me..."

Tuning out, Ana smiled and nodded at points she hoped were appropriate. The last thing she needed to hear about was Ciara's sex life.

When it was clear that she wasn't going to get much more than gushing about how wonderful Esteban was in bed, Ana finished off her bun. "I should go. I wanted to find out if anyone knows what's going on with all this snow."

Ciara frowned but nodded. "When you do, let me know. I hate the thought of leaving, but we can't stay here forever, can we?"

Nodding, Ana stood. "Sadly, we cannot. I'll see you later."

Just as Ana reached the door, Esteban strode past. The look he gave her didn't feel malevolent. It did make her feel a little dirty, considering he was sleeping with her friend and he was clearly checking her out. Other than that, he didn't give her any impression beyond being a cad.

He smiled, and all at once Ana noticed several things. One was that Esteban was wearing makeup. That in itself wasn't that odd. She'd noted that a lot of men wore makeup in this world. Usually the insanely vain men who felt they had something to prove. Or hide.

It wasn't until his smile faded that she realized he had been trying to hide a bruised eye and another patch of color on his cheek.

Then there was the slight limp as he walked past.

He'd been the one to attack her in the gallery.

Turning on her heel, Ana hurried past him and back to Ciara. She had no idea what she was going to tell her friend. All that she knew was that she needed to get her away from him.

"Ana!" Ciara grinned at her approach. It faded quickly when Ana didn't return the smile. "What's wrong?"

Maybe she was jumping to conclusions? "I noticed that Esteban was limping."

"Apparently he had a mishap in the gym last night. He's a clumsy boy, I'm afraid."

"He gets hurt often?" How did he manage that? Ciara wasn't with him every minute of the day. Could he be a useless thief wannabe?

"All the time. He can't walk and breathe at the same time." Ciara rolled her eyes as she took the last sip of her drink. She cast her gaze behind Ana. "Was he coming in?"

Ana shrugged. She was more concerned with trying to figure out Esteban. "I don't know. He walked straight past me."

"I guess I'd better go find him before he injures himself again. I swear, I need to wrap him in cotton wool to make sure something doesn't get fractured."

"All right." Ana absently air-kissed her. "Be careful."

Ciara gave her a quizzical look before walking out.

Ana wasn't sure if she was right about Esteban being the other one in the gallery. She couldn't very well start hurling accusations about the love of Ciara's life without at least having a little proof.

Looking for inspiration, Ana wandered through the hotel until she found herself in the lobby at the front desk. And, of course, Cabral was there, as well.

At her approach, he grinned. "Fancy seeing you here."

She forced a smile, as tight as it was. "How nice to see you again, Mr. Cabral. I was just looking to see if there was an update on the weather."

"As was I."

They both turned to the receptionist who had been within earshot and had to have heard what they'd said.

"According to the weather service, the storm should let up any time now. In my opinion, it should let up by tomorrow. I'm afraid I can't be more accurate than that." He smiled apologetically. "However, tonight there will be a continuation of the ball, if you're so inclined."

"Thank you." Her heart had started galloping at the thought of finally get out of the holding pattern that she'd been in the past few days.

Cabral noticed her excitement. "Have you been that bored here? You've lit up like a Christmas tree at the news of the party continuing."

Ana did her best to calm herself. "You have to agree that it gets a bit dull wandering around any place for days on end, even one as beautiful as this."

"And here I thought it might be due to the company you're keeping." Cabral winked at her. "If you find yourself in need of a new distraction, all you need to do is let me know."

She mutely watched him leave, refusing to reply to his remark. Just thinking about spending any amount of time with him made her skin crawl.

What she needed was to confirm the receptionist's prediction and tell Rhys. As she headed up to the penthouse, Ana pulled out her phone to check the weather predictions on several services to try to get an idea of what was going on.

She took the long way around, making sure to walk slowly and let people see her. If the one who attacked her was around, they might take the bait and make themselves known. Then again, they could have simply been reacting to her presence in the gallery and not even known who she was.

Still, it couldn't hurt to see if she had anyone following her.

Ana wandered every inch of the hotel accessible to the public, but besides a few looks and cajoling smiles, she didn't notice anything out of the ordinary among the bored hotel patrons.

She wasn't sure if not seeing Rhys around anywhere was a reason for concern or not. It was a big hotel. It was entirely possible that she'd missed him. Or he and Christine were currently naked in a bed somewhere.

It was a thought Ana wasn't equipped to deal with.

Having Rhys back in her life hadn't been expected, but after spending time with him again, she had to admit that she enjoyed it. He was the man she remembered and then some. But the situation they had found themselves in was anything but regular. If she had ever imagined settling down with a man and having his child before, she certainly hadn't thought this was how it would be.

It could have been worse. He had learned the truth about her and hadn't freaked out, too much. He was capable and appeared to be interested in being a father.

Ana wanted to accept that things would work out for them. But how wonderful would he think being a dad was when he had to live with the reality of a child? Sure, Eric was adorable in photos and on video, but he wasn't like that twenty-four-seven. What child was? Did Rhys understand that?

Spending time with Rhys again was wonderful, magical even, but she couldn't let herself lose sight of the fact that she was a mother first. As much as she cared for Rhys, her baby came before all else. If he didn't understand that, then it was probably best he stayed out of their lives.

Another thought that twisted her insides. A life without Rhys in it was as unpalatable as it had been before. Knowing that he was alive and that if he didn't stay in her life this time it would be by his choice made her stomach roll.

Cold dread inched along her veins. It was definitely a possibility she would have to talk to him about. She couldn't usher him into Eric's life just to have him walk back out again.

There was so much to consider on top of everything that was going on at the hotel. Ana took a deep breath and continued on her trek.

If Rhys ripped her heart out again, she would survive. She had once before and, if it came down to it, she would again.

Disheartened, Ana fought back the emotions. Later. She could fall apart after the job was done.

By the time she reached the door of penthouse, the sky outside had changed from a dull gray to almost anthracite in color. The walk had hardly been aimless, however. Ana had plans for most, if not all, eventualities and a backup for each when she opened the door.

What she hadn't been prepared for was what she saw on the other side.

"Rhys?"

Ana picked a path through the rose petals as if they were mines. The scent of them suffused the air in the room with a cloying sweetness. Long white candles glowed from almost every surface.

He stepped out of the shadows with a glass of champagne in each hand. What knocked the breath from her lungs was the way he looked in an impeccably cut tux.

"You look like James Bond."

"I thought you might like it." He lowered his head for a kiss before putting a glass in her hand.

Still stunned, Ana let him do both. "What's going on?"

"I figured since this would more than likely be our last night in this place, we should do it right."

"How did you…?"

"You're not the only one who can go around asking

questions." He took her hand and led her to the table.

More rose petals, more candles, an incredible-looking meal, more romance. That he had taken time to do this... Ana couldn't help the wave of emotions that swamped her. Strongest of them all was the overwhelming love that she had been trying to keep at bay. She was in love with Rhys again. Still. Always had been. That would never change.

The smile dropped from his face when he caught a glance at her expression. "What's wrong?"

"Rhys..."

"It's too much, isn't it?" He put his glass down with a loud clink. "I knew I shouldn't have—"

The last wall she'd erected between them shattered. Ana grabbed his head and dragged him down for a deep, biting kiss. "Rhys, I love you." She kissed him again before pulling back. "I can't fight it any longer. It terrifies me, but I know it's right. If there's any man out there that's perfect for me, it's you." She stared into his eyes. "I know it's crazy and it couldn't come at a worse time... Tell me I haven't screwed it all up."

Rhys froze for a moment at her admission before he wound his arms around her and held her tightly when she would have pulled away. "I love you, too." He kissed her again as if to make sure that she knew it was the truth. That she could feel it. "There's no one else for me."

He sucked and licked her bottom lip as he drew back. "We'll get through this and when we're looking back at this five—ten—years from now, it's going to be a great story to tell Eric."

Her jaw dropped. "That his mother, the thief, and his dad, a secret agent of some clandestine agency, worked together to save his life from a crazed criminal? It's going to give him nightmares."

"So we'll wait fifteen years, then, just to be safe."

He said it so calmly, so assuredly, that it seemed almost reasonable. Inevitable, even.

Ana could almost picture them maybe having another

baby, growing old together in the millhouse. Peaceful, quiet lives.

If she could wish for one thing, that would be it.

No more looking over her shoulder, crazy plots or worrying who was trying to work what angle. She wanted to relax, live life and be loved.

By the man currently holding her.

If she couldn't have all that, Ana could at least have this one last night.

Looping her arms around his neck, she pulled him down for another kiss. "How hungry are you?"

"For you?" Rhys picked her up and swung her up into his arms. "Can't be satisfied."

That was all Ana needed to hear. As much as she loved seeing him in the tux, she needed it off — now.

On the way to the bedroom, she managed to get rid of the tie, the jacket and unbuttoned most of the buttons.

Rhys lowered her to her feet next to the bed and began reverently peeling off her clothing.

Ana, however, had other ideas. She didn't want to be treated like glass. What she wanted was all of Rhys' fire and passion. She needed him to burn away all the doubts and fears.

Pushing him back, she quickly divested herself of clothing before tearing his off and pushing him onto the bed.

Straddling his hips, Ana kissed him again, willing him to understand what she needed.

Chapter Thirteen

Rhys sensed the turmoil coursing through her, the need to shove everything aside until it was just the two of them here, now. He was more than willing to do whatever she wanted of him in order to help her escape. Even if the moment was fleeting.

Rolling her under him, he pinned her arms to the bed then ravished her mouth. He alternated hard biting-kissing with long, deep caresses with his mouth and tongue before moving lower. Eventually, he had to let go of her hands to explore with his mouth and tongue.

He loved the little sounds of pleasure that escaped her as he moved over her body. Especially when he closed his lips over her peaked nipples and sucked. Rhys would never grow weary of the sigh that came from her. Flicking his tongue over her, he drew her into his mouth again, enjoying the way she arched into him wantonly. As if he was the only one who could give her this much pleasure.

As far as he was concerned, he was.

Taking the other nipple into his mouth, Rhys grazed his hand down her side. Her skin was a marvel. Soft and silky, so smooth. He loved the feel of it against his. Over her hip, across her thigh, he trailed his fingers toward his goal.

Ana parted her thighs for him, eager for his touch. That she was so keen for him pumped his ego more than anything else could have. His cock throbbed, but he wanted to taste her first.

Rhys took a long moment to toy with her clit, lightly grazing it with his fingertips. He knew it was enough to create some sensation but not enough to edge her toward climax. It would frustrate her, maybe even infuriate her, but it would be worth it.

"Rhys, more," she moaned. Ana rocked her hips, trying to get friction.

Who was he to deny her anything? Slowly, he slid his fingers lower. Ana was already slick and probably aching for him. His mouth watered as he caught her scent.

When he looked at her, her eyes were hooded and she watched him avidly, waiting for his next move. He could see she was impatient, but fighting her impulses. How much it would take to make her control snap?

Holding her gaze, he parted her folds and pushed two fingers into her. Crooking them on the way out, he grinned as her hips lurched from the bed when he plunged them back in.

Rhys couldn't restrain the chuckle at her squeal after he added his mouth and tongue to the equation. He kept a steady rhythm with his fingers while changing it up on her clit with flicks of his tongue and gentle suction. It didn't take long for her cries to transform from intermittent exclamations into a long keening litany of his name while she bucked under him.

He continued his ministrations until she sagged into the bed and dragged his head away. Rhys took it as his cue to slide up her body and plunge into her.

As tired and oversensitive as she was, Ana arched upward to meet his thrust, crying out lustfully once he hit the sweet spot deep within her.

Gripping her hips, Rhys drove into her again and again, setting a punishing pace that threatened to incinerate the room along with them.

He didn't care. All he cared about was taking her to the peak and crashing over with her.

He didn't expect Ana to have the presence of mind to push him off and straddle him. Taking him deep inside her again, she controlled depth, angle and pace. Rhys felt utterly — wonderfully — used.

Still, he wasn't going to let her take all the control. Closing his hands over her hips, he tugged her and thrust upward with every down stroke. Ana started to tremble, her jaw slack as her orgasm built.

Needing to come with her, Rhys sped up his thrusts, grinding his pelvis into hers, feeling himself harden even more.

Then there was the tell-tale flutter of her inner muscles, his name on her lips. And Rhys exploded.

He had no idea how long they lay there, but by the time he managed to regain his senses, the candles had burned low. He'd forgotten he'd even set them in there. Rhys had hoped that they would end up in the bedroom after dinner. This had worked out much better.

He gazed at her dozing in his arms, lying flat on his chest where she had collapsed. In fact, he hardened inside her again whilst she shifted.

Ana stretched languorously against his hard chest, enjoying every bit of sensation she derived from it. The resurgence of his erection inside her told Ana that he had no complaints. However, as much as she would love to go another round with him, they had more pressing matters to attend to.

Just one more second…

Ana lay languid for a moment longer. "We need to get up."

"Oh, I'm already up." Rhys shifted his hips, sliding himself deeper into her.

She savored the flicker of awareness her already taxed body responded with. "As much as I would love to take advantage of that, we have things to do."

He grumbled something but rolled his hips a couple of times before she managed to slide off him.

Hoping a kiss would salve his pride, she leaned in for one. Rhys took advantage and hauled her up against him, kissing her thoroughly then he leaned back. "No matter what happens tonight, remember I'm on your side. I love you. Everything that I do is for you and Eric. Don't lose sight of that."

Ana's heart almost burst from hearing the words, but dread also seeped into her system, souring his confession. What was he preparing to do for her? For their child? "Same goes for you."

He held her gaze.

She cupped his cheek. "I know things can and probably will get crazy. We can handle it. But I want you to be careful. Take whatever precautions you need to. I can't lose you again."

Rhys's expression turned a little melancholy as he reluctantly let go. "If you have any pregame rituals…"

"I do, as I'm sure you do, as well." Ana smiled at him. "Are you willing to add a shower to yours?"

"Absolutely." He slid from the bed and offered his hand, which Ana took without hesitation.

The shower was silent but filled with glances, caresses and kisses as if they were memorizing each other. Ana couldn't shake the feeling that this could be the last time they would be able to do this.

Rhys didn't seem to be doing any better than she was. His kisses were tinged with desperation and something too close to sadness.

She had to believe they were going to come out of this better, stronger. Eric would need them both, and Ana would do whatever was in her power to provide him with everything he needed.

That included saving his father from himself, if need be.

Once they were out, Rhys dried her off after which he tucked a towel around his hips. Ana needed to get him out of the funk before they left the penthouse. There was nothing worse than a fatalistic attitude going into a job. She'd know people who had practically predicted their own deaths and even when they had been able to see it coming, had done nothing to stop it because they'd felt it was fate.

She needed Rhys to know that fate had no hold over him.

Wrapping her towel around them both, Ana pulled him down so he would look her in the eyes.

"Promise me you're not going to do anything crazy."

He met her gaze and held it unwaveringly. "I'm going to do whatever I have to."

"Do whatever necessary to come back to me."

Rhys only responded with a slow kiss that sent tingles skittering through her.

He was going to say something else but was interrupted by a trill of his phone. With a regretful glance, he stepped out of her embrace and went in search of it.

Ana followed him into the room to find him speaking quietly. He caught her gaze and quickly ended the call, but the expression on his face was lighter than it had been.

"I take it you have some news."

"That was Christine. She'd taken me up on my advice that the gems might be safer elsewhere for a while."

Ana stared at him. How could he do that? "You told her to move them? I'd just figured out a way of getting the diamond!"

He cupped his hands over her shoulders. "Calm down and listen." He waited for her to meet his gaze again before continuing. "Think about it. I've discussed it with her and they have contingencies for this sort of thing."

Fuming, Ana glared at him. "Which are...?"

That was when Rhys grinned. "They are replacing the ones in the gallery with replicas and storing the real ones in the hotel vault."

How was that better? She hadn't had the chance to even look at the hotel's own security. He knew how much they had riding on this and the abbreviated timescale... "I'm going to kill you."

He pecked her on the nose. "After all that love talk?" Rhys pulled out the all-access key card, a piece of paper with Christine's room number and a small pouch. "We've got this. And" — he tapped her head — "this. Between the two of us, we can circumvent pretty much any system. And with the gems out of the gallery and in a less public location..." Rhys let her fill in the rest.

Ana untied the drawstring to the pouch and tipped the contents into her hand. The diamond that tumbled out filled her palm, and at a quick glance was identical to the one she'd been staring at the past few days. Both the move and the replacement diamond did make a couple of problems easier to deal with. But what were the chances that a hotel like this would have a vault that would be as easy to walk into as one in a small town bank? She needed to see what she was up against before she could decide whether or not to throttle Rhys.

"And one last thing."

"There's more?"

Rhys ran his hands up and down her arms. "I got it into her head that the most valuable pieces would be best in her suite's safe. Since they would be separate and no one would be the wiser with the copies on display, they will be totally safe."

And ripe for the picking.

"Pretty good, huh?"

She begrudgingly gave him a smile.

Rhys nudged her. "Admit it, I'm a genius."

"Maybe, a little." Much of the pressure ebbed away. A safe in a suite was going to be child's play. All they would need was a distraction...

Ana looked at Rhys. Was this why he seemed so down? "You're going to distract Christine..."

His face was carefully blank. "Can you think of a better way?"

"Just how distracted are you going to make her?"

"Distracted enough." He bumped her forehead with his. "Ana, I told you, I'll do whatever it takes. But I'm planning on taking her to dinner at the big restaurant with the huge windows" — he checked his watch — "in about thirty minutes. That should give you a couple of hours to do what you need to. Unless you think you might need more time."

"I think I'm insulted." Ana brushed her lips against his. "Are you sure you haven't strayed to my side of the law before?"

Rhys deepened the kiss before replying "If I had known you were on the other side I would have jumped the fence years ago."

She couldn't help the bubble of laughter. "Sweet-talker."

For the first time she could remember, Ana felt a sense of surety. That she had found her other half, that Rhys was a true partner in life. Whether it was professionally or personally, he was her man.

Rhys smiled at her, though the light in his eyes betrayed the fact that he was a bit confused. "What?"

"I'll tell you later." Right now they had to get ready.

Rhys took his cue to leave so she could prepare. Knowing that he probably had his own routine before he went to work eased her conscience. The last thing she wanted to do was upset him by kicking him out, but she needed to focus. Rhys was able to demolish her concentration simply by being in the room.

She quickly dried off and retrieved her clothes from the bag. Far from the finery that she'd worn lately, the black cargo pants, sweater and boots she usually wore for this sort of thing seemed overkill for a simple safe-cracking. It might do well to fit in with her surroundings this time.

Ana chose a casual outfit consisting of an over-sized cream sweater and dove-gray jeans and a pair of Balenciaga boots. She looked like a typical patron of the exclusive Totally Five Star Hotel and yet she'd managed to conceal whatever she needed under the sweater, in the pockets of the jeans and even the boots.

After she'd wound her hair up in a loose bun and had applied enough make up to look like she'd made an effort, she decided she was ready.

The woman reflected in the mirror was serious, focused, but what she felt inside was less so. Did she still have the skill required? Had she lost her nerve since becoming a mother?

Ana glared at herself and mentally caged all the doubts in the back of her mind. She *would* do this and come out the other side unscathed with a smile on her lips and the diamond in her hand.

She didn't look in on Rhys. Not only did she not want to intrude on whatever prep he was doing, but she didn't want to see him looking good, getting ready for a date with another woman.

As it was, she had enough distractions to worry about. The last thing she needed to do was fixate on what he was doing with Christine.

Not that she had anything to worry about.

Not at all.

It was her vivid imagination that was the problem.

Taking a deep breath, Ana pocketed the diamond and walked out of the suite.

She took a long looping path through the hotel as she waited out the time. When there were four minutes left to spare, Ana stood outside the restaurant and waited. It didn't take long for her to spot Christine and Rhys approaching. They seemed cozy. They weren't touching as they walked, but the body language of both were of two people who were into each other.

Guilt pricked her gut, but she ignored it. What they were doing was a necessary evil.

Rhys whispered something to Christine that caused her to giggle and blush. The intimacy of the move manifested a surge of jealousy, making Ana bite her lip to keep from snarling. It was a ruse. She knew that. It didn't stop her from reacting instinctively, however.

Just as she was about to turn away to head up to Christine's suite, Rhys turned at her and held her gaze for a fraction of a second. He knew exactly where she was without having to search, as if he was fully aware of her presence at all times. As if he sensed her. That and the look itself reassured her somewhat.

The knots in her stomach eased when Rhys and Christine entered the restaurant but immediately bunched up again when she backed up into a solid form behind her.

Murmuring her apologies, she tried to skirt around the man, but he curled a big hand around her upper arm, holding her securely.

"Are you okay, Countess?"

Cabral. Why did he have to show up now? Ana pulled her arm out of his grasp. "I'm fine, thanks."

He lifted an eyebrow quizzically. "Not going to dinner?"

"No."

"Does it have something to do with your ex? You were staring at him as if you wanted to kill him."

Uneasiness in her already alert system tensed her entire body. Ana needed space between them. She needed to get out of there. "I've got to go."

Cabral nodded understandingly. "It's a good thing the snow is letting up, then, isn't it? You can get out of here that much sooner. Away from him."

"That's the plan. I think I'm going to pack." Ana tried to edge away, but he stopped her again. Keyed up as she already was, Ana was on the alert. Was he going to try something?

He caged her with his arms, and she shifted her stance, ready to take him down if he pushed her too far.

Cabral held her gaze as he slowly reached into his jacket pocket. Ana released the breath she had been holding when he pulled out a card. With a smug smile, he slipped it into her hand. "Forget about him. What you need is someone else. Call me when you're ready for a real man."

Ana took several deep breaths as he walked away. Muscle by muscle, in tiny increments, she relaxed. At least, as much as she could at the moment. As smarmy as he was, she was beginning to think that his less-than-savory reputation was no more than gossip. Probably perpetuated by the man himself to create a veil of danger and mystery. It was cheap and low, but what did she expect? There were women who went for that kind of man and he was merely catering to them.

Pulling herself together, she quickly made her way back up the hotel. Cabral had cost her a few precious minutes. When a mere second or two could mean the difference between success and failure, minutes were far too much time to waste.

Still, she had to appear calm and casual, even though all she wanted to do was race to the suite and tear it apart until she had the diamond in her hands.

The trip up to the suite was long and agonizingly slow. She knew cameras were witnesses to her every step, so she made certain to avoid movements that would give away her intentions.

Behaving like she belonged, like she was doing nothing out of the ordinary, was key.

Without hesitation, she entered Christine's suite and immediately headed to the bedroom, knowing the safe would be in the walk-in closet exactly as it was in her room and Rhys'. Thank goodness for the lack of imagination in hotel planners.

She grabbed a spare sheet from the small stack of spares on the shelf and spread it out over the floor to catch any possible debris. Then she focused on the safe.

Running her gaze over the silky metal front, she examined it. Should be easy enough. The electronic lock would have at least a million permutations but, as with most hotels of this caliber, it would have the ability to be reset so a patron would have their own individual code, which in turn made it easier for the hotel to manage. When the patron left, the code would reset for the next one. A wonderful setup for high turnover. And it made Ana's life a little easier as well.

If only she had stored something in hers so she would have had a starting point.

Or had already done a job in a Totally Five Star Hotel before.

Had she had more time to prepare for this scenario, Ana would have had her tools with her. In this case, she had to rely on skills she'd picked up over the years and a lot of luck.

Ana nimbly inputted a factory set combination as she brainstormed other possibilities. Her hope was that the hotel wouldn't have error lockdown activated because of the headache it would create for the staff. When, after the first combination failed and it didn't lock her out, Ana smiled a little as she continued to work.

She didn't know Christine, so specific dates were out. Her suite number might do it. It was easy to remember and, if a patron couldn't do that much, all they had to do was look at the door.

Tapping in the second sequence, Ana heard a soft shuffling then what sounded like the door closing. Was Christine back? There was nowhere for Ana to go. How the hell would she explain being in Christine's suite?

Ana held her breath and stepped behind the door. Maybe whoever was there would miss her and leave none the wiser.

"Anastasia. I know you're in here."

Ciara? What the hell was she doing here?

Ana stayed where she was as dread trailed icy fingers down her spine. Had Ciara followed her? How had she gotten into the suite in the first place?

Most of her questions were answered when the elongated silencer of a gun came though the closet door first.

On pure instinct, Ana kicked the door hard, knocking the gun out of Ciara's hands.

"Bitch!"

Ana took a blinding fist to the face before she countered with one of her own to Ciara's jaw. She kicked Ciara's knee and sent her tumbling to the floor. Faster than she could recover, Ana kicked her gut and punched her face again, incapacitating her for a moment.

Ana stepped back. Where was the gun?

Her search wasn't quick enough. Ciara had recovered swiftly and kicked her ankles out from under her. Wind knocked from her lungs, Ana punched the woman as she climbed on top of her. Ciara savagely slammed her fist into Ana's face, her throat, her chest, anywhere she could reach.

Despite Ana's defensive maneuvers, Ciara managed to land a few well-aimed blows that hurt like a son of a bitch. She had to give her credit for getting the drop on her, as lucky as it was.

Ciara snarled and changed tactics, wrapping both hands around Ana's neck, proceeding to attempt to squeeze the life out of her.

The skinny bitch was stronger than she looked. With her vision beginning to blur, Ana slammed her fist back solidly in her eye then pushed up from the hips to knock her off.

Wheezing for breath, Ana hauled herself up to her hands and knees. "I'm going to kill you."

"Not if I kill you first." Ciara grinned viciously at her down the slightly misaligned silencer of the gun.

Even as negligible as it was, Ana noticed it immediately. It must have been damaged when she'd kicked the door into it. Ana hoped that she would try to shoot her and that it was damaged enough that the backfire would be more than enough to take care of Ciara.

Ana sat up, spitting the blood that had pooled in her mouth. "Why?"

"The same reason you're doing it."

"If you think you have any idea why I'm here, you're wrong."

Ciara laughed. "I know that you're here to get a diamond for Marco Valente." Her laughter rang again when Ana glared at her. "I also know that if I kill you and take the diamond to him, he'll appreciate it very, very much."

She thought Marco would fall for her if she did this? Ana couldn't even begin to fathom the insane rationale that would lead her to that conclusion.

Ana needed to keep her talking. Wanted to find out what

was going on. "What about your darling Esteban?"

The bark of laughter from Ciara was cold. "I was trying to train up the idiot, but I guess some people clearly aren't cut out for the job."

Ana wasn't sure if she wanted to know what Ciara had done to him or not.

"So now what? You kill me, leave. And then...? People are going to be asking a lot of questions. The security cameras alone will tell the authorities everything they need to know to take you down."

"Please. Just because you didn't have the foresight to deal with the cameras doesn't mean I didn't."

"And my body?"

Ciara scoffed. "Who gives a shit? I'll have the diamond, my man and we'll live happily ever after."

If Marco ever had a match, this was her. Ciara was as bat-shit crazy as he was.

"You need me to get the diamond."

Ciara scowled skeptically. "I know all about you, Ana *Meier*. That everything you've told me about your life is bullshit. I also know that the great Ana Meier could crack a safe like that in a few minutes."

She pressed the gun against Ana's cheek as she searched her pockets. Ciara yanked out everything she could find, including the pouch. Undoing the ties with her teeth, she then dumped the diamond onto the floor. Triumphant, she sneered at Ana and ground the muzzle harder into her face. "I thought so. What other lies are you going to tell me?" She quickly stuffed it back into the pouch and stuck it in her pocket.

A little spark of optimism flared in Ana's chest. "None. Just take it and go."

The twisted expression on Ciara's face was every bit as ugly as the woman inside. "And you're simply going to let me go? You actually think I'm stupid enough to believe that?"

"And you really think I'm going to turn you in? I can't say

anything because I'm involved." Ana pointed at her blood on the floor. "My DNA is in here. I'd have to explain why I was here with you, bleeding all over what's sure to be a very expensive carpet."

Ciara seemed to think it over, so Ana kept talking.

"Marco will appreciate you bringing him the diamond. And on top of that, I'd owe you one."

"I do like the idea of that…" The press of the gun lessened.

Hope slowly seeped into Ana's veins. "Let's get the hell out of here, then, before someone finds us."

"I said I liked the idea." She pulled out a knife she had hidden in her boot and dragged the cold flat of it down Ana's cheek, her neck, over her stomach to press the edge against the top of her leg. "But I never agreed."

With a vicious grin, she sliced it across Ana's thigh.

Ana cried out through gritted teeth as fire burned from the cut. Closing her hands over it, she fought from screaming as the searing pain blinded her vision for a moment.

"Don't be such a baby. I didn't hit anything vital. Only enough to keep you here to take the heat." Ciara kissed her forehead then stood up to give Ana a wink. "I'll give Marco your love."

With that, Ciara did a triumphant little dance and twirled from the room.

Cursing how stupid she had been, Ana retrieved the pocketknife she hadn't been able to reach before and sliced strips off the sheet and, with shaking hands, wrapping the swaths around her thigh to stem the bleeding. Ciara had been right when she'd said it wasn't too deep, but it was bad enough. When she was sure the bandages would hold, she cleaned her hands as best she could.

When she caught up with Ciara, she was going to pay.

As she studied the aftermath, Ana had never been so glad for high-thread-count sheets in her life because it had caught her blood and kept it from staining anything underneath.

If Marco thought he had the diamond, he might leave without a fuss. That was the hope, but it wasn't a risk she wasn't willing to take.

It was better to have the real one as a backup, just in case.

Ana dragged herself upright and propped herself up with a hiss. Fighting the nausea, she jabbed the hotel room number into the keypad. There was a beep and the lock disengaged.

Ana deftly tugged the door open only to slam it shut again in fury.

Rhys covertly checked his watch. Ana should have been in and out by now. In case she wasn't, he'd buy her a little more time.

"I was surprised that you wanted to go to dinner tonight. I thought I saw something between you and the countess."

He sighed heavily. "It's complicated."

Christine nodded sagely. "Relationships often are." She nibbled on a baby carrot as she studied him.

The last thing he wanted to talk about was his and Ana's relationship with another woman. They had come a long way the past few days. Though they still had a lot to work out, he was optimistic about their future. But talking about it with someone else was sure to be something that Ana wouldn't appreciate.

"So were the event organizers concerned when you decided to move the gems?"

Christine gave the people near them a quick glance. She leaned forward and whispered, "A little, but when I explained the danger, they were glad to do it. Though they wouldn't let me keep any in my suite."

Rhys nearly choked on his food. "Really? Why's that?"

"They agreed the logic was sound, but they feel the vault is much more secure."

"It's their prerogative, I guess." He might have sounded nonchalant, but Rhys' mind was reeling. Ana would be furious and had probably jumped to the conclusion that he had conned her.

Could he blame her? He would probably think the same

thing.

But she would be livid. What would a mother desperate to save her baby do in this situation?

Besides burn down the hotel around him in the belief that he'd betrayed her?

Christine's voice tore into his thoughts. "Do you feel like checking out the ball after this?"

"Maybe." Definitely not. He had to find Ana before she did something crazy.

"Are you all right? You look a little pale."

He forced a smile, knowing it would add authenticity to his act. Though it wasn't a complete farce. Rhys did feel sick, but not for any reason Christine would think of. "I think I might have eaten something that disagrees with me."

Concern was immediate on her face. "Want me to walk you up to your suite? Call the doctor?"

He waved her off and gave her a brave smile. "I'll be fine. Nothing a little rest won't cure. Please stay, order whatever desserts you like. Have them bill it to my suite."

Rhys pushed himself to his feet, accidentally knocking off her purse. Retrieving it, he gave her a half-hearted pat on the arm before walking from the busy dining room. The moment he was past the entryway, he picked up the pace. Where would she be?

He headed up to Christine's suite first, hoping she would be there.

"Ana?" He had taken Christine's card when he'd knocked her purse off the table so entry was no problem. Rhys headed straight into the closet to find it empty. A closer inspection of the safe and the area around it didn't give him any clues.

After leaving the card on the floor by the door to make it look as though Christine had simply dropped it, Rhys dashed through the halls. What would Ana do next?

Get the diamond, of course.

But would she go to the vault or the gallery?

If he were her, he would have probably come to the

conclusion that he had lied about everything and had gone to the gallery for that diamond. Which meant that the real one would be in the vault and ignored. If Ana wanted the real one, it meant he would have to be the one to get it.

Rhys ran through a number of scenarios as he made his way through the halls. The vault, as far as he knew, was a room filled with safety deposit boxes in a secure room behind the front desk.

What he needed was something that would divert attention from him as well as Ana. There was no way he would leave her without backup and in danger of getting caught as he did this.

But what?

Whatever it was, it needed to draw attention from the ball and the front desk.

And he needed to come up with it fast.

Rhys reached the lobby, his concerns becoming moot. The fire alarm, or at least what he figured was the fire alarm, went off. Even the alarms in this place were classy. Whatever it was, the sound stopped people in their tracks.

"Everyone please stay calm and make your way to the ballroom." Hotel staff appeared and pointed people in the right direction.

Rhys sincerely hoped that Ana was on her game because there was nothing he could do to help her now besides get the real diamond.

He waited until the stragglers were out of sight before rounding the counter to access the computer there. Rhys quickly deduced the password for the hotel's computer system, rewound and froze the security footage for that area then accessed the logs for the vault. From there, it was simply a matter of unlocking the door and the one to the right box. All from the computer.

God bless whoever had come up with the idea of linking everything into one system.

Rhys pushed open the door and stepped inside. The walls were lined with little metal doors of varying sizes, smallest at the top and biggest at the bottom. He headed straight to the medium sized one with a green light.

As expected, it required a key to get into the box itself. There wasn't the time to finesse it open. What he wouldn't give for a crowbar right now.

Rhys went back to check out the desk. There had to be a backup master key card around somewhere.

He grabbed one that he figured was, and whatever other cards he could find, and brought them in with him.

Swiping the first card didn't work. Neither did the next three. There was no room to wedge the cards...they'd probably just snap anyway. But there was a keyhole.

Dashing back to the desk, Rhys searched for a tubular security key.

Under the desk was a ring with several keys on it. One of those had to be it.

Rhys willed himself to breathe and slowly try the keys one by one. Rushing and making mistakes wasn't going to help anyone.

Finally, one allowed itself to be inserted and turned.

Pulling the box out with care, Rhys flipped open the lid to reveal its contents. As Christine had said, the gems were all their in separate little containers. Finding the diamond was easy. He only wished he had the fake to swap it with.

Stuffing it in his pocket, Rhys rearranged the containers, closed the box, exited the room, put the keys back in place and reactivated the security feed.

Now to find Ana.

Hurrying into the ballroom, Rhys kept an eye out for Ana and Christine. Seeing neither, he made his way through the crowded room toward the gallery in the hopes of finding Ana.

When he entered the room, he found it just as packed as the ballroom—with the exception of the podium that was supposed to hold the diamond.

Chapter Fourteen

Ana shoved clothes and the soiled sheet into her bag then dialed her phone.

Javier answered on the third ring. "Ana. Tell me some good news."

"I've got it, but I doubt I'll be able to get a flight out yet. Think you can find me an insane pilot to pick me up from the hotel?"

"Done. Serge should be able to get to you within the next half hour."

Perfect. "Tell him to track my location."

"I will. See you soon."

He would.

Ana hadn't seen Ciara anywhere, so figured she had found a way to reach out to Marco. She needed to get there to head her off before Marco's unpredictability kicked in.

And it would if he found out the diamond was a fake.

The one she had retrieved from the gallery was a good fake, but without the formula was still a fake. Ana didn't have any choice but to take this one to Marco. She didn't have time to waste with the vault, especially not when the alarm had gone off.

She would just have to make it work.

Ana stared at the bed a moment. What to do about Rhys? He'd given her bad information. But had he known it was bad when he'd passed it along? Ana didn't want to believe that he had lied to her, but there was always a small chance that he had willingly led her astray. But why? He knew what was at stake.

The old doubts stared to chip away at her confidence in

him.

She would deal with them — him — later.

Right now, getting Marco out of her life and her son's was more pressing.

Without a backward glance, she walked out.

She headed to the other end of the hotel, as far from the ballroom as she could get, and exited the hotel. The snow was deep but the front of the hotel looked as though it was being cleared periodically.

Definitely large and clear enough for a helicopter.

Her phone buzzed. Ana swiped the screen.

Be there in 5.

Not that she expected Serge to let her down. The man was an expert at driving anything with wheels and without. Nothing short of a full-blown hurricane could keep him grounded. His skills behind the wheel had saved them all at one time or another and had earned him a place in Ana's inner circle.

She would owe him big for this one.

Ana could vaguely hear the helicopter approaching when she also heard an all too familiar voice behind her.

"Sounds like my chariot is here."

Ana turned to face Ciara. "I figured you were the type to have things ready to go. Didn't you know that stealing someone else's ride is in bad form?"

"And I thought you had enough brains to know when to give up." Ciara calmly pulled the gun out and trained it on Ana. "I guess I'll have to do more persuading this time."

Ana didn't have to look to know the helicopter had landed behind her. She needed to go now before anyone came to investigate the noise. The quickest, though completely insane idea, was that her only chance of getting away was goading Ciara into shooting and hope that the silencer was damaged enough to give her a few precious moments to get away.

No time to try to figure something else out. Ana shrugged. "I'm getting out of here. You're going to have to kill me to take my seat."

The feral smile that Ciara gave her sent chills skittering down her spine.

"That's the idea."

With a prayer on her lips, Ana turned and limped as quickly as she could out of the lobby and into the snow.

She was still close enough to hear a click then a frustrated scream behind her, but she kept up her dash to the helicopter. When she closed her hand around the handle, euphoria rushed through her.

Pulling the door open and grinning at the man who was at the same time urbane and a dead ringer for a lumberjack, she threw her bag inside.

Serge shouted something she dimly heard over the deafening rotors a split second before someone grabbed her by her jacket and dragged her back.

Tumbling into the snow, Ana caught a glimpse of Serge drawing a weapon. But her vision burst with stars as a blow to the back of her head dazed her.

Ana managed to dodge the next strike. She grabbed Ciara's arm and swung her into the side of the helicopter.

Taking advantage of Ciara's guard being down, Ana slammed her knee into her back and smiled grimly at the satisfying crunch. She didn't have time for this. Ana punched her twice more then opened the door again.

Ciara wasn't deterred. She clawed her way up Ana's legs and dug her nails into her wound.

The blinding pain lanced through her, tearing a scream from her throat.

Ana dropped back to the ground, using the downward momentum to drive her elbow into Ciara's face.

Bloodied but still grinning, Ciara kicked Ana's injured thigh, sending her to her knees.

Gripping Ana's hair, Ciara pressed her cheek to Ana's. The scent of the other woman's blood roiled Ana's stomach.

"I'm going to kill you, then your kid."

The threat ignited a deadly fury in her blood. Ana wrapped her wrists with Ciara's hair and twisted as she pulled, throwing Ciara over her shoulder into the snow.

There was no way Ana would let her get away to carry out her threat. They would end this now.

Ana stood, turning to watch Ciara push herself back up to her feet and draw her knife again.

The light glinted coldly off the blade as Ciara lunged.

Ana stabilized herself as best she could, but the momentum of the other woman slamming into her threw her off balance and drove her to the ground once more.

Marshalling her strength, Ana rammed her forearm against Ciara's neck, forcing her back then punched her again with her other fist, pushing her back further.

The crazed anger on Ciara's face impelled Ana to fight harder. Only one of them was going to make it out of this. Ana would make sure that it wasn't Ciara.

Ciara slashed the knife through the air at her face, missing by a hair's-breadth. Ana managed to knock it off course as she swung it back. Ciara was getting sloppy from either anger or fatigue, which helped, but blood loss was slowing Ana down.

As much as Ana twisted and fought, Ciara wasn't giving her any openings. Finally, Ciara slammed her fist into the wound on Ana's thigh over and over until Ana couldn't see past the spots flaring in her eyes or feel anything but the pain lancing through her.

Incapacitated from the pain, Ana struggled weakly but knew Ciara had gained the upper hand.

Glaring at down at her victim, Ciara gripped the handle of the blade with both hands. And held it over her head ready to strike.

She licked the blood from her lips with an exaggerated swipe of her tongue. "This is going to be so good."

Taking the chance, Ana surged forward, knocking her back, and kicked her farther away with her good leg.

Ciara leaped at her again.

Then she stopped. The smile on her face faded into confusion just before she dropped face first into the snow.

Standing at the door of the hotel, Rhys lowered his gun.

Ana stared at him for a moment. At least he had helped that much.

Let him deal with Ciara and the fallout here. She had to get home.

Fighting back the tears, Ana pulled herself up into the helicopter and shut the door.

Rhys watched as Ana painfully climbed into the helicopter and shouted something at the pilot. He put his gun away and immediately took off without a second glance. Rhys' attempt to get close to it was thwarted when the vehicle lifted off and created a mini tornado of wind and ice that forced him back.

Shit.

Well, that dispelled any question of whether or not she was angry with him.

He stared at the slowly disappearing helicopter for a long moment. Rhys then glanced down at the woman, who was trying to push herself up to get the knife despite the gunshot wounds to her shoulder. The pilot must have taken a shot when he did. It had been the only moment they could have gotten a clean shot. He smiled grimly at the various injuries he assumed Ana had given her.

She hadn't taken it lying down, either, from the state Ana was in when she'd gotten on board the chopper.

What the hell had happened?

He kicked the knife away before using the same foot to turn her over. "Where is she going?"

She coughed, splattering blood on the snow and gasped, "Why should I tell you?"

"Because it's not too late to save you."

"And if I don't tell you, you're going to let me die?" She spluttered more blood. "That'll never happen. You're law.

I can smell it."

Rhys' leash on his temper snapped. That was his woman and his child out there in danger. As far as he was concerned, she was getting in the way of his protecting them. A temporary roadblock that he'd drive straight over if he had to.

No more games.

Leaning on one knee, he stared her down. "Not any longer. Tell me and I'll get you medical attention. Or" — he closed his hand around a gash on her arm and squeezed — "we can do this the fun way and I can *persuade* you to tell me then leave whatever's left of you to slowly and painfully die here in the snow." He snarled at her. "Either way, you're *going* to tell me."

Ciara hissed a breath when he let go. She nodded wearily. "It's a village. An hour's flight away."

She muttered a name, but it was enough.

Rhys pulled out his phone and made a couple of calls as he searched her for weapons. He scowled when he found a familiar pouch. Taking it, Rhys shoved it in his pocket as he stood to leave.

Ciara spat blood on his shoe. "You said you'd help."

He barely spared her a glance as he checked his phone. "And I've called the authorities who will see to your injuries when they get here."

Rhys waved security over to deal with her. He had other places to be.

Ana touched down at a clearing near the millhouse. She had wanted to catch Marco off-guard and sneak into the house. It had seemed like the best tactic at the time, but as she and Serge approached she noticed that the house was too dark. Too still. In fact, it was deathly quiet.

Were they too late?

What Ana loved about the little house was that it always seemed brimming with life. In the spring, the flowers and plants turned it almost postcard perfect. Birds and small animals were abundant in the area, even in winter. But now there were no lights in the windows, no smoke from the chimney.

The house looked dead.

Ana pulled out her phone and dialed Javier.

After two rings, her call went straight to voicemail. Ana leaned against a tree to steady herself as she studied the implications of him not answering his phone.

Serge stared into the darkness. "Doesn't feel right."

"It doesn't." Ana shoved her phone back into her pocket. "Javier isn't answering and the house looks abandoned. Something must have happened."

But what? Ana's mind ran riot. Had they gone somewhere safer? Had Marco gotten to them?

Bile started to rise in her throat. If he'd hurt Eric…

Ana took a step, but Serge held her back.

"What?" She immediately started to scan the scene.

"I thought I saw movement in the windows."

The seeping cold of the wet and frigid environment had nothing on the icy dread that froze her veins.

Ana shoved him off. "I have to get in there."

Serge grunted but gripped her again as he continued to scan the area.

Ana took a few slow breaths to try to calm herself. She needed to think clearly and panic wasn't going to help.

Serge's low, rough voice broke into her thoughts. "You must have some other way of getting in. Did you think this would never happen?"

It was something Ana hoped would never happen but had considered it a possibility. "I have a way in. Follow me."

Being a millhouse, the cottage was set alongside a small waterfall where the watermill was powered. Instead of a mill, there was now a deck over the waterfall, but what most people missed was the little door that was accessible a few steps above the waterline at the shore below.

Even Ana had missed it the first two viewings, hidden

thanks to the long grass and shrubbery that was a godsend now.

Without a second thought, Ana led the way into the shallow water. Memory allowed her to pick the safest path. Still, it was slow going and the frigid water soaked her jeans and stabbed pain into her legs with icy claws.

By the time she reached the door, her hands were shaking and not solely from the cold. Fighting to make them work, she managed to get her key in the door. She was never more grateful than in that moment that she had upgraded the door months before. Where there once had been a heavy, creaking, rotting wooden door, there was now a near silent, waterproof door.

Ana waved Serge in while she disabled the alarm.

The familiar scent of the house eased her nerves. She was home. Minutes from now she would be reunited with her baby and all would be right with the world.

Just as soon as she got a certain man out of their lives.

Ana slowly followed the well-worn path up the stairs and pushed the door open a crack. Dead silence. Since having Eric, it was a sound that filled her with dread. There was always a something to hear with a child around—even when he was asleep she could hear him breathing over the baby monitor.

The eerie silence now pricked the hair at the nape of her neck.

Where the hell was everyone?

Where was Marco?

Ana waved Serge to follow. The darkness didn't bother her since she knew every inch of the house. She walked past the sideboard she'd found in Milan, careful not to brush the statue of Shiva that liked to snag clothing if she wasn't paying attention. She directed Serge around the rug from Morocco that had one corner that refused to lay flat.

But as they made it to the living area, a voice stopped her dead.

"You can stop sneaking around, Ana."

His familiar voice alone was enough to make her snarl. When she would have lunged at him, the crack of a silenced shot stopped her. It was a split second before she realized there was no pain. It was Serge who'd been hit.

The lights went on, and she immediately checked over the man at her side. Serge had taken a bullet to the shoulder. Through and through from the looks of it. Ana bunched his clothing and pressed it to both sides of the wound as Serge stoically took the pain with nothing more than a grimace. The glare he gave the other man, however, held a multitude of promises. It widened into fear when he motioned Ana to look.

She turned to find Marco holding Eric, who slept peacefully with his head nestled in the crook of his neck, clutching his ever-present teddy bear. Ana didn't know what she wanted to do more — tear Marco's smug head off or take her child into her arms.

The rage she experienced went further than only at the man in front of her. Where the hell were Javier and Sara? The two people she trusted most to protect her son had failed miserably, leading to Marco holding him as if he were his own, letting him wander around her house as if it were his.

Ana eyed the man threatening her son. Marco could have been handsome if he wasn't completely deranged. His dark brown hair lay flat on one side and stuck out on the other and his clothes were rumpled. In contrast to his tan skin, he had a scar on his throat that ran from under his ear down his chin and into the collar of his shirt. She would have assumed that he had been torn from bed. But there was that manic glint in his eyes that told her Marco knew exactly what he was doing and that she needed to get Eric away from him as quickly as possible.

She held her arm out. "Give me my baby."

"Give me the diamond."

"The baby first."

Marco smiled. The toothy grin was reminiscent of a shark

and it only served to boil her blood more. "I like that you aren't afraid of me." He let his gaze sweep over her, as if he were considering her for something. "Since you're here and Ciara isn't, I'm assuming you have disposed of her." His smile was approving. Almost proud. "She wanted so much to best you, you know. Boasted that she would take down the great Ana Meier. I told her that she didn't stand a chance. I'm glad you proved me right."

Ana ignored him. "Baby, please."

The smile slowly evaporated. "You should learn how to relax a little, my dear. You are really trying my patience." He lowered his head and sniffed Eric's hair. "Babies have this amazing scent, don't they? So clean. So pure. Like everything else about them. Until we fuck them up, of course."

Ana edged closer, fighting the urge to launch herself at his throat. She couldn't risk hurting Eric.

"I'm thinking of getting myself an apprentice down the line. With your boy's pedigree, he'd be an excellent student. I could teach him all the things he'll need to know to be a master thief and demolitions expert. The three of us could work together as a team."

Yeah, right. Ana could imagine what Marco thought was needed to become a master thief. Especially when he had no idea how to steal a pen from a bank let alone anything of value.

"I'm here to get my baby back and to give you the diamond. That's it. I do this and we're done."

Marco gazed almost lovingly at Eric, something that made her stomach crawl.

"I can't get over the thought that he could have been mine, you know."

Roaring filled Ana's ears.

She wasn't sure what delusion he was under, but he had never been in the running. She recalled saying something to the effect of hanging out together outside of work—she'd only said it out of an obviously misguided need to be polite during a conversation once. And that had been before she'd gotten to know what he was really like. Had he twisted it in his head into something more? He was out of his mind. She would have informed him of the fact, but he was still talking.

"I watched you…and him, you know. Not the kid…well, him, too…but you and his dad. It was disgusting how happy and in love you were with him."

Marco had been there and watched them in Positano. The fact sunk in like a rock tossed into the ocean. It made her skin crawl to think that he'd been witness to what was the most romantic time of her life.

The bombs of information exploded in her head one by one as he continued to speak.

"I had those urchins bring you a gift that last night." Marco fluttered his free hand. "Call it a congratulations or a housewarming gift. Whatever. What I hadn't planned on was the little bastards' curiosity."

Ana covered her gasp with her hand. He had been the one who had caused the explosion? Did Rhys know he was responsible for his partner's death?

She couldn't stop the anger from putting a tremor in her voice when she snarled, "Those were defenseless children."

He scoffed. "At least they had a purpose for a few measly minutes. Then they had to go and get greedy."

Bile burned the back of her throat. "So you were trying to kill us?"

"Him more than you." Marco shrugged. "But if I got rid of him, you'd freak out and I didn't want to deal with the hassle so…" He looked down at Eric again and shrugged. "I guess it was one of those 'if I can't have you then no one will' kind of things."

As if the thought of taking lives so callously had been no big deal.

"No more." She couldn't stomach hearing anything else. Ana tugged the diamond from her pocket and held it out pinched between her thumb and forefinger so he could see it. "Take it and leave us alone."

Marco grinned, baring his perfect teeth. "Beautiful." He held his hand out for her to drop it into, but held tight to the baby.

"Baby first."

Tutting, he shook his head. "You must understand my need to verify its authenticity."

Ana deftly tossed the gem then snatched it out of the air to grip it in her hand. "And you must understand my need to hold my child."

He rolled his eyes but nodded.

Ana gently took Eric from him. On the step back to stand next to Serge, she tossed Marco the diamond.

Kissing Eric's hair, she checked him over to reassure herself that he was unharmed. Satisfied when she found nothing amiss, she glared at Marco. Now to find her friends. "Where are Javier and Sara? Also, I'd appreciate if you left the house how you found it when you leave." Not that it mattered since she wasn't going to be returning. As far as she was concerned, everything had been tainted by his presence.

He blinked and turned his gaze to her as if he'd just noticed that she was speaking. "Not so fast. I have to verify that this is the diamond I'm looking for. You are to stand there until I do."

Desperation to get away clawed at her. "Of course that's the diamond. I spent days busting my ass getting it to you. I'm not going to stand here while you stare at it, trying to decide if it's authentic or not."

Another roll of his eyes. "God, you *have* been out of the game a long time." Marco pulled his phone out of his pocket and took a picture of the diamond, edge on. Three times he did this. Until he had photos of each edge. He swiped the screen and gave her a lazy glance as he waited. "In a few seconds, I'll know if I have to kill you both."

She needed to get the hell out of there before he found out she had lied. Staying as outwardly calm as possible, she mentally went through her options without tipping him off to her unease.

As Ana tried to figure out an exit strategy, a creak on the floorboard she'd been meaning to fix came from the kitchen an instant before a shadow appeared behind Marco.

"I've got the real diamond, Marco." Ana's heart stopped as Rhys stepped into the light and held up the gem. "If you want it, let Ana and the others go."

"And the other one arrives. It took you long enough." Marco sighed heavily, tucking away the phone and retrieving his gun in the same move. "Why should I believe you? For all I know, you're just playing white knight to her damsel in distress." He flicked the gun toward Ana.

"The last thing I need is *his* help," spat Ana.

The gun lowered. Marco's interest had been piqued. "Do I sense a rift between the lovebirds?"

She didn't bother meeting Rhys' gaze. Instead, Ana glared at Marco sullenly.

Marco crossed his arms, leaving the gun poking out over his bicep. "This should be interesting."

Rhys clenched his jaw. "I did some things I'm not proud of. Some of which Ana doesn't approve."

She couldn't help the snort of derision. "He's proven himself a liar and doesn't like to be called out."

"I am not." Rhys pointed at Marco's pocket. "Am I lying when I say that's not the real diamond?"

Marco gave them one more appraising gaze before dropping it to glance at the screen of his phone. His surprise was quickly masked. "You tell the truth."

Holding the diamond in his hand up to catch the light, Rhys said, "And now when I tell you this is the diamond you want?"

Nodding, Marco eyed him. "I'm a bit more inclined to believe you."

He waved it in the direction of Ana. "So get rid of them and you can have it."

Marco calmly placed the fake on a nearby table. He held

out his hand. "Prove it and I let them go."

Rhys kept looking at Ana, but she stubbornly refused to meet his gaze. He did, however, catch a few glimpses at the little boy in Ana's arms. He appeared healthy enough asleep against Ana's shoulder. A strange pride came over him that his son was as heavy a sleeper as he was. What other similarities were there?

His son.

The need to get him and Ana out of there, away from Marco, intensified.

He had a plan, and if Ana would only spare him a glance, he might be able to signal her to play along. But she kept her gaze frustratingly averted.

Marco held his hand out and Rhys really had no choice but to give him the diamond for verification.

Marco went through a tedious routine of taking photos. Rhys had arrived just in time to catch the end of Marco's verification process last time and had studied him from the shadows.

Marco had one gun. No back-up. Without the two incapacitated babysitters in the other room and the wounded helicopter pilot next to Ana, they were two against one. Or at least two individuals against one. Not to mention what waited outside.

Anger flared in his gut when Ana continued to refuse to look at him. This wasn't a game. They were fighting for their lives, the life of their child, and yet she insisted on behaving like a petulant little girl.

So he made another mistake. He was human. It wasn't like he could control everything. If he had that ability, things wouldn't have turned out as they had. Far from it.

The seconds ticked by as Marco's gaze ricocheted between them, completely amused by their display, if his expression was anything to go by.

The phone beeped and the smile on his face grew. "Well, you're not a liar after all."

Ana scoffed and Rhys had to clench his fists not to respond.

"You two should really consider counseling, you know." Marco admired the stone under the light before slipping it into the front pocket of his trousers. "It might save your relationship."

Rhys glared at him. "Look, I don't need your relationship advice. You've got what you wanted. Let Ana and the baby go."

"So touchy." Marco turned to Ana. "You know, if you're sick of this guy…"

Ana smirked. "You have no idea. All he's done is lie to me and use me when it's convenient."

"That's such bullshit, Ana. You know it wasn't like that." Rhys wanted to throttle her, but she kept going.

She stepped closer, her voice staying deadly calm. "Really? Then what was it like? Like you lied about your death?" She stepped in between him and Marco. Stood toe to toe with him. "Like you lied about your identity?"

"I told you why I had to do that."

"As far I know, you've probably lied more." Ana eyed Marco. "Maybe I do need a real man."

Rhys's entire body seized up from shock at that. What? And Marco, that son of a bitch, had the gall to grin and wink at her! "You don't mean that."

She finally met his gaze and gave him a heavy-lidded glance. "And if I do? Would you fight for me?"

That thought…it wasn't worth thinking about. As his gut churned at the thought of Ana with Marco, it slowly dawned on him. She had given him a look when she'd said it—pointedly held his gaze.

Ana was trying to tell him to fight Marco.

Not that it would take that much prompting. Rhys balled his fist and, with all the pent-up rage, smashed it into his face.

Serge pounced at the same time, disarming Marco and turning his own gun against him.

Ana bounced Eric a little when he woke from the commotion but still managed to come across as though she would quite easily tear Marco limb from limb with her free hand. "Get out of here, Marco. You got what you came for. Leave us in peace."

Rhys got in his way. "We can't let him leave with that diamond."

Ana held his gaze. "If it guarantees he will leave us alone, I'm willing."

All eyes turned to Marco, who shrugged. "I don't see why not. I hardly need the hassle of a kid or a woman in my life right now."

Ana's eyes glittered with anger as she stared at him. "Get out of here."

Marco sidestepped Rhys with an almost apologetic smile and walked out of the front door.

He sagged with relief the moment the door closed behind Marco. Ana let out a rush of air.

"You're going to let him go?" Serge put the safety back on the gun and tucked it into the back of his jeans. "Just like that?"

"He doesn't have the diamond. Ana held up a glittering stone." She laughed a little when both men turned to look at the diamond still on the table.

Patting down his thigh, Rhys chuckled. "You picked my pocket. How did you even know I had the other fake?"

"I could see the outline and I figured if Marco thought he had the real one, he would leave. I only wanted him away from Eric. We can track him and make sure he doesn't do this again, and now we have a little time to play with."

She was good. Rhys was impressed with how quickly she'd figured things out and worked it to her advantage. But he did have one last thing to reveal.

"No need to worry about Marco." He turned his gaze pointedly at the door Marco had just used.

They opened it at the same moment the police surrounded Marco.

"You came with the cavalry." Ana smiled up at him. "At least you thought ahead. Have you seen Javier and Sara?"

He pointed in the direction of the room he had seen them in. Rhys was completely confounded by her change in attitude. "So...you're not mad at me?"

Ana led the way through the hall. "No. I was for a little while until I figured out what had probably happened, but I needed you to believe I was to fake out Marco. If he saw us as disjointed rather than united, he wouldn't be as guarded."

And she had been right. Of course, she'd worked with Marco before and would know how to manipulate him better than he would have.

They quickly found Javier and Sara. The sickening scent of ether was barely detectable in the air. Marco had obviously piped it into the bedroom.

"We should get them out of here." Ana stayed well back, keeping Eric away from the harmful fumes.

Serge, being the bigger man and stronger, even with an injured shoulder, helped Javier while Rhys picked up Sara. On the way out, he couldn't help but notice the amused smirk on Ana's face.

"What?"

"I'll tell you later. First I want to watch Marco be arrested." She wedged her free shoulder under one of Javier's arms to help Serge as they made their way out of the house. Eric started to fuss, but Ana managed to continue half-carrying Javier while calming him. She was incredible. The baby was restless and refused to be soothed, however. Who could blame him with everything going on around him?

Thankfully, Rhys had thought far enough ahead to make sure that there was an ambulance waiting among the police cars.

Marco stood among the cops, staring at the group walking out of the house as if he didn't have a dozen guns trained on him. "Congratulations. You got me."

As paramedics rushed to help them with Javier and Sara,

Eric let out a wail. Ana rocked him, but he wasn't going to be pacified.

He watched as she took a blanket from the ambulance and wrapped it around him, talking and snuggling the baby but there was no stopping the tears.

Ana approached Rhys, bouncing the bawling baby on her hip. "Are you sure you're ready for this?"

Was he? Rhys took in the little red face, the tears, the snot, the screaming, and couldn't imagine being anywhere else.

He nodded. "Absolutely."

The smile on Ana's face lit up the night. "Great. Then hold him for a second while I go and find his teddy. He must have dropped it. No one will get any sleep if he doesn't get it back."

She nuzzled the baby. "Eric, this is your daddy. He's going to hold you for a bit. I'll be back as soon as I can, sweetheart. I promise."

Placing the baby in his arms, Ana pressed a kiss to their cheeks. His first then the baby's. She readjusted his arms to make sure the baby was supported then gave him a teary smile. "I've dreamed about this moment."

Too afraid to let go of his son, Rhys nodded and tapped his forehead to hers. They had so much to talk about. To learn and relearn. "Hurry back."

"Won't be long." Ana gave him a watery smile as she turned to hobble into the house.

Rhys looked at Eric and found him staring up at him with big eyes that matched his own. "Your mum sure is amazing."

The baby babbled something Rhys took as agreement. For the first time in a very long time, Rhys felt free. He *was* free. Now that Marco was in custody, he could do anything he wanted with his life. And he wanted to spend it with Ana and Eric.

Rhys noticed that the baby's squirming seemed to be directed at trying to get something on the ground and looked to see his bear. Kneeling, he picked it up and whipped it to knock off bits of grass before handing it to Eric. Ana would be happy that it wasn't lost when she came back empty-handed.

"I need you to come with us to Paris, Agent Stone." The officer in charge approached him. "You will need to file the required reports and eye-witness testimony that will help us put him away for good."

Rhys gritted his teeth. "How long would that take?" Days, maybe. He hoped that a week or two would be the most the man would reply with.

"I can't tell you. It could be a few weeks or a few months to get things sorted out."

He truly wanted to see this through. No matter how much he wanted to stay with Ana at the moment, he had to make sure that Marco went to prison for a very long time.

"We will also need the others as well..."

Rhys's vision narrowed. That was one thing he hadn't anticipated. He'd been so concerned with taking down Marco and getting back on Ana's good side that he hadn't thought of what the law would need on the other end of the equation.

Ana and her friends weren't going to like this.

"Where are they?"

"Who?" Rhys looked at the ambulance first. It was empty. Another quick scan revealed Serge was nowhere to be found, either.

And Ana?

His gaze returned to the man in cuffs. The feral grin on Marco's face turned Rhys' blood to ice. What was he grinning about?

"Say goodbye to your girlfriend." He mockingly lifted his hands and pressed a button on the little black device.

"No!"

Officers jumping to restrain him were too late.

The house exploded in a blinding ball of orange and red flames.

Rhys turned and covered Eric's tiny body with as much

of his own as he could as they were thrown by the force of the blast.

They landed not too far away, Eric's screams muffled by the ringing in his ears. Rhys carefully uncurled himself from around his son. When he was sure that he hadn't suffered any lasting damage, Rhys dared a glance at the wreckage of the house. All that was left of the house was burning. The tongues of fire licked the dark sky in mocking slow motion.

"Ana!"

Chapter Fifteen

One month later

Rhys stared out of the window at the sprawling city, at the darkening sky that lay like a shroud over everything. Springtime in England was a misery. Not that he could tell what season it was, really. London's weather was drearily monotonous all year round. It fit his mood perfectly, however. It was probably why he had returned in the first place.

The dark skies and sullen atmosphere suited him.

It was time for a change, though.

But he was a father now. He had to get out of the dark mood and be a good dad. Even if it meant faking it until he found his way. So far he didn't think he'd done too badly. They were both still alive and without injury. Eric even seemed happy enough. He had everything he could ever need and more. Rhys would call that a triumph by any gauge.

He turned to look at the monitor and saw that Eric was sleeping peacefully in his crib. It was amazing how easily the baby had taken to him. Good thing, too.

All the shit with Marco had been done and dusted. It had been quick and painless. It was one of the few times lately that Rhys had felt indebted to the agency. Had he been regular law enforcement it could have dragged on for months, maybe even years. But now Marco was behind bars and cement and would be for a very long time.

And finally Rhys could rest.

Only he was edgy. He couldn't relax. Rhys wanted to

believe that Ana was still out there. The way she'd said she wouldn't be gone long. The way her friends had disappeared. It couldn't be a coincidence.

That, and there had been no trace of her in the remains of the house. And he had been through every inch of the debris and had sifted through the singed remnants himself.

Rhys hoped beyond hope that she was just sorting things out on her end then would come to find him.

That hope was waning, however, week after day after hour, minute, second... What if she decided that life as a thief was better than being a mother? It was no picnic, but he couldn't let himself believe it. He'd seen her with Eric. She loved him. All the shit she'd gone through for him...

Or maybe he was being delusional.

He stalked his way into the kitchen to make himself an espresso. By his watch, Eric would be waking for a cuddle in an hour, a habit he'd picked up shortly after arriving in London. Far be it for Rhys to deny him that.

He had bought the apartment some time ago, hoping that Ana would join him in it one day. It was bigger than two people needed, but he liked the space. It was modern and high above the city. Rhys liked it because it put space between him and the rest of the world.

The hope was that Ana would like it, too.

Guess he'd never know now.

As the espresso brewed, he leaned against the counter and stared at the wall on the other side of the room.

In the middle of his musing, there was a light knock on the door.

He checked his watch. Who the hell could it be at this hour?

Rhys pulled open the drawer nearest the door and keyed in the code to unlock the gun there. Taking it out, he then held it behind his back as he hurried to open it before they knocked again and woke Eric.

And found a woman with long flame-red hair looking down the hall on the other side. Disappointment flooded him.

Wearily, he rubbed his face. "Can I help you?"

She turned to face him and his heart stopped.

"Ana."

Rhys didn't question it. He crossed the space between them. Gun still in hand, he cupped her face and kissed her before she could say anything, hoping that it would say everything he needed to.

Ana sank into the kiss. Feeling him, tasting him again, was incredible after being apart for so long. It might have been only a few weeks, but it felt like years.

When they had to separate to refill their lungs, Ana held on. "I'm so sorry. I—"

He stopped her apologies with a shake of his head. "I don't care. You're here. You're alive. It's all I need to know.

Rhys took her hands and dragged her in, redepositing the gun as he did.

Ana gave the room a quick survey then met his gaze again. "How has Eric been?"

"Better than I have." Rhys ran his hands over her cheeks once more before leading her down to the hall to where the baby slept.

Ana leaned in to kiss him, caressing his curls as she stood back. "He's changed so much and it's barely been a month," she marveled.

As much as she needed to cradle her baby, she wanted his father more in that moment.

"Rhys…"

He'd already taken her hand and was leading the way to the master bedroom.

Rhys fingered the long waves that cascaded over her shoulders. "This is new."

"I thought I should disguise myself, in case anyone was watching your place."

"*Our* place," he corrected.

"I was hoping you'd say that." Heart singing, she ran her

fingers along the waistband of his sleep trousers.

"Just one thing."

Ana's heart stopped then lurched to life again, beating ten times faster when he plucked the wig from her head and tossed it aside.

Running his fingers through her real hair, he whispered huskily. "I want you. Only you. The real Ana."

She grinned. "You have her."

Rhys picked her up and lowered her to the bed so he could look at her as he peeled her clothing away.

Slowly, piece by piece, he tugged the fabric away until she was laid bare before him.

Ana wanted him skin to skin with her as soon as humanly possible, but he stood and stared at her as if he were committing her to memory.

If he wasn't going to come to her…

She started to sit up, but Rhys shook his head. "Just give me a second." He leaned down to run his hands over her skin, stopping for a long moment at the scar on her thigh, tracing the ugly gash from end to end.

His touch was better than nothing, but it was far from enough.

Ana squirmed. "I'm starting to feel self-conscious."

"About what? You're amazing. You have an incredible body."

She let her gaze glide down his body and back up to meet his eyes. "How about you let me see *your* amazing body."

Chuckling, he quickly stripped down and held his arms out. "Better?"

"Much." He was a gorgeous specimen of a man. All hard muscle and sinew. And his cock… She craned her head to the side "One thing would make it better."

He grimaced. "Ouch."

Ana laughed. "What would make it better would be if it was pressed against me."

Rhys immediately climbed in and dragged her to him. "Never let it be said that I left a lady dissatisfied."

The sensation of his bard body skin to skin with hers was delectable. But Ana wanted more. She wrapped her leg around his hip and rolled so that he was over her.

Rhys didn't need to be told twice. Pressing a kiss to her throat, he adjusted himself and pushed into her inch by delicious inch.

Ana arched under him wanting, needing, as much of Rhys as she could get. She hadn't been sure what to expect when she'd arrived. But this was much better than anything she could have anticipated.

He had missed her as much as she had missed him. He didn't care about her reasons, only that she was with him again.

She would explain everything, tell him everything, later.

Rhys set a hard driving pace that belied his desperation as much as it sated hers. However, once he drove her over the edge, he slowed his thrusts. Softened his kisses.

Leaning back, he brushed her hair out of her face and gazed into her eyes. "I thought I'd lost you." His voice was husky, rough with unshed tears.

"Never." Ana understood how he felt. If she could have done the night over she would have warned him more. Made sure he understood that no matter what she would be coming back to him. But there hadn't been a plan. If there had been, she would have made sure to spare him the devastation.

But that was the past.

The future spread out before them was clear of lies and mistrust. Without the past holding them back, Ana was positive that what they had would grow stronger over time.

Rhys held still, pressing himself deep, as far as he could go. "Swear to me there will be no more lies, no more deception."

She arched under him, wanting him even deeper. "I swear it."

"I promise you the same." He sealed his oath with a searing kiss. "That I will do whatever it takes to make you smile and never have to worry about anything or anyone ever again." Rhys punctuated his words with a roll of his hips.

He picked her up and twisted around so that her shoulders and head were propped up against the wall and she straddled his thighs.

Ana wrapped her legs around his hips and rode him with Rhys' help, using the wall for leverage. He pulled her down with every upstroke, maximizing every sensation, sending shafts of pleasure lancing through her body.

Biting her lip, Ana fought to keep quiet. There was little hope of holding anything back when the pleasure crested. There was just too much emotion. Too much joy.

Rhys wound his hands in her hair and dragged her mouth down to meet his when she hit her peak and her cries refused to be held back.

He plunged into her again and again until she quivered around him once more and he couldn't hold himself back any longer.

Mouth to mouth, their bodies wrapped around each other and trembling, they stayed that way for several long minutes while trying to catch their breaths.

Rhys smiled at her as he lowered her to the bed and they melted, still entwined, into the sheets. "Give me twenty minutes and I'll promise you a whole bunch of other stuff." He joked, but Ana knew that Rhys meant every word of what he had said.

Chuckling, she nestled closer to him. "How about you just lie here and hold me for a while?"

"Try to stop me."

* * * *

Ana woke. It took her a moment to remember where she was. A slow smile spread over her face as she recalled how she had been lulled to sleep.

Sliding a hand over to the other side of the bed, she found

it cold.

"Rhys?"

Even after all the promises and the fantastic sex, he had left? Had the whole thing about him being okay with her disappearance been just a charade?

No. She wasn't going to let her mind wander down that road.

Ana kicked the tangle of sheets off her legs and was about to go check on Eric when she heard it.

Over the baby monitor, Rhys was talking to Eric.

"Hey, little guy. Thought I heard you moving around."

Eric burbled something that made both her and Rhys chuckle.

"Mummy's back. She's missed you. I'm sure she'll be in here shortly."

More babbling came from the monitor along with the sounds of a baby being changed. Ana wanted to witness that for herself.

After throwing on a robe, she crept along the hall until she stood in the doorway of Eric's room. Rhys had gotten the hang of changing a squirmy baby and managed it quite quickly, before putting Eric back in his crib.

After Rhys disposed of the diaper and dimmed the light he turned to find her watching.

Admiration, she hoped, was clear in her smile. "You're a pro."

He gave her a lopsided grin and shrugged. "I'm a fast learner." Rhys wrapped an arm around her shoulders. "I hoped you'd sleep through that."

She shook her head. "I've missed too much as it is." Ana dragged him along with her as she entered the room to pick up Eric and give him a snuggle. He happily tangled his fists in her hair and yanked to show his mother how delighted he was to see her again.

Ana laughed and tickled him, more than delighted to be with him once more.

The excitement soon turned into yawns as the early hour

caught up with him.

Ana put him back in the crib and rubbed his back until he fell asleep.

Once she tugged the sheet over him, Rhys smiled. "Want to get back in bed?"

It was still dark, but Ana was awake now. "You can if you like. I'm going to make some coffee."

"Tell you what. I'll get the coffees if you slip back into bed."

"It's a deal."

Ana padded back to the room and straightened the sheets. Dropping the robe, she slipped back into the expansive bed. So far what she'd seen of the apartment had been lovely. The décor might have needed more of a feminine touch, but Rhys had done a good job.

She could definitely see herself living here.

It was a quick few minutes before Rhys returned with a couple of steaming mugs. He placed them on the end closest to him then slid into the bed to wind his arms around her with a happy sigh.

Ana gladly did the same.

"This feels good." Rhys' voice rumbled through him and into her.

"It does. But I still have to tell you where I've been."

His arms tightened. "You say that as if whatever is on your mind will change this."

Ana twisted so that she could look Rhys in the eyes. "I hope it doesn't."

Rhys settled them back but didn't let go. "Tell me."

"First, I'm sorry I dropped Eric on you like that. After everything…I felt that he was safest with you."

Rhys laughed. "It certainly didn't feel that way in the beginning."

She smiled. "I know the feeling, believe me."

"And I kind of get how you felt seeing that building go up when you thought I was in it."

"Sorry about that, too."

"Don't be. All of this gave me a glimpse of what the past two years of your life has been like. I don't know how you held it together, to be honest. Four weeks and I was a gibbering idiot."

"You did fantastically. I knew you would." Ana brushed her lips against his.

Rhys kissed her with fervor. He pulled back after a long moment. "So where did you go?"

"I had a few things to take care of myself." She looked down at her thigh. "Then I had to make sure that no one was going to bother us." Ana craned her neck back to gaze at him. "If you're happy for there to be an 'us', that is."

"Of course I am. I can't even express how ecstatic I am that we have the chance to be together. Now we can be a real family."

His words made her smile. "So you're glad to be a dad, then?"

"Are you kidding me? Eric is amazing. Brilliant, even. Keeps me on my toes."

Ana chuckled. "I'll bet."

Rhys nodded. "I can't wait to have more like him running around."

She gawked at him. "He's not really running yet, is he?"

"He's certainly trying."

Rhys handed her one of the coffees, which she accepted gratefully. She took a tiny sip and smiled. "You remembered exactly how I like it."

"With far too much cream and sugar." He sipped his inky-looking drink and sighed. "That's more like it."

Ana nestled against him and, for the first time in years, truly relaxed. "Remember when we used to wake up like this in Positano?"

"All the time."

"And that interlude on the beach…"

"Where you took total advantage of me?" He turned to rest on his hip, facing her, at the same time letting her know full well how remembering the interlude on the beach affected him.

Ana shifted her thigh and 'accidentally' brushed his growing erection. That earned a groan from him.

Rhys put his coffee down. "Why the trip down memory lane, Ana?"

She smirked at him. "Well, remember after the first couple of weeks together there it was pretty clear that we were hooked on each other?"

"Of course. Though I think I realized even before that. Probably from the moment I saw you I knew that my life wouldn't be the same."

Her grin couldn't be stopped. "I think it was the same for me too."

Rhys took her coffee and set it aside. "So…"

"I'm getting to my point." She took a long breath. "After the early days, we stopped using condoms…"

He nodded. "We're both clean and you were on the pill."

"And, well, I must have missed one in that lust-filled haze because I think the beach trip was when we made Eric."

"Yeah?" A grin grew over his face. "It *was* kind of magical."

"It was." Her smile grew, though it was a little shaky.

Rhys snapped out of his awestruck reverie when he noticed her grin. "What?"

"Well. You've been dead for the past couple of years and I had no interest in falling into bed with anyone else."

He lowered his eyebrows. "You already told me that."

"So why would I need to be on the pill during that time?"

Ana waited for his brain to catch up to what she was saying. While they'd been in Chamonix they had slipped back into old habits and hadn't even considered taking precautions.

Rhys' eyes widened as he ran his big hand up her thigh to caress her stomach "Are you telling me…?"

"I hope you were serious about wanting more babies running around."

"Hell, yes!" He dazedly stared blindly at the other wall

for a moment before his grin threatened to split his face.

Ana laughed at his expression. "You're gloating."

"Damn right I am. Another baby with the woman of my dreams? And this time I'm here right from the start. What's not to love about that?"

Rhys rolled her under him as he kissed his way down to her stomach. He gave it a gentle caress of his lips then he met her gaze with a huge grin.

"What?"

"You have to admit that I'm pretty potent to knock you up while you were on the pill and this time after only a few days."

Laughing incredulously, Ana tapped him on the head until he looked at her again. "That's what you're thinking?"

He kissed her belly before sliding back up to do the same to her lips. "Among so many things." Rhys radiated happiness just as Ana knew she was as well. "But most of all, the one all-consuming thought is, that I love you, Ana. So very much."

Feeling as if her heart would burst, Ana brushed her lips against his. "Right back at you, Rhys."

Epilogue

Three months later

Ana sat on the veranda and smiled as she watched Rhys and Eric running on the beach with the new puppy that Rhys had insisted every growing boy needed.

He'd also convinced her that they needed a honeymoon, which was how she'd ended up on a beautiful beach enjoying a glorious evening.

Rhys definitely knew how to get his way.

Ana didn't mind at all. His surprise wedding gift had been a villa on the beach in the Bahamas. As far as gifts went, this had to be one of the best she'd ever been given. The others—she rubbed her little bump as she watched Rhys and Eric—were pretty spectacular as well.

She took a moment to enjoy the play of sunlight on the glittering ring on her finger.

"You're looking awfully smug, Mrs. Stone." Rhys carried Eric now as he approached and gave her a kiss. Not to be outdone, Eric gave her a sloppy one as well. Then, of course, the puppy had to join in.

She beamed at her boys. "I can't think of any reason not to be."

Rhys looked at the hand she still had on her stomach. "My little boy playing up?"

Ana rolled her eyes. "Not at all. And I keep telling you, this one's a girl."

Covering her hand with his, Rhys smirked. "We'll see." He put Eric down. "Show Mum the shell you found."

Eric held up the little shell and chattered something about

it then dropped it in her hand with a hearty laugh.

Ana wound an arm around him and dragged him in for a cuddle. "Come here, you little monkey."

He squealed with delight before giving her another kiss.

"Ana! Rhys!"

Ana turned to find Javier and Sara heading down the beach toward them.

Rhys picked up Eric and helped her out of the lounge chair.

She gave them hugs and pecks on their cheeks. "What are you two doing here?"

Javier shook hands with Rhys before he turned to Sara. "You'd think she was unhappy to see us."

"Not at all!" Ana led the way into the villa. "Make yourselves at home. Can I get you something to drink? To eat?"

"I'll get coffees." Rhys handed Eric over to Ana then left with the puppy in tow.

"Relax, will you?" Sara took Eric from Ana's arms and made growling noises to the delight of Eric. "We're only here to visit."

Ana couldn't help the smirk. "So it's 'we' now, is it?"

Her friend blushed. "Not in the same way you and Rhys are quite yet." Sara patted Ana's stomach. "But yeah."

"I'm glad." It had been a long time coming and Ana was glad that they had finally come to their senses.

Ana waved her friends to sit. "Rhys is out of earshot, so why are you really here? It's not Marco, is it?"

"No, nothing like that." Javier patted her shoulder. "And if it was, we'd take care of him long before he got anywhere near you again. We owe you...and him."

She nodded, understanding how they felt.

The need for retribution was a powerful one, but Ana knew that she was done with that life. Blessed with good friends, an amazing partner, babies and a puppy, her life couldn't get much better.

Sara nudged her. "By the way, Serge will be along shortly

as well."

Ana arched an eyebrow. "Oh?" If the three of them were here together...

Sara sighed. "I'm sure you've already guessed—we're looking at a...job...in the area and wondered if we could pick your brain."

She was done with that life with the exception of maybe dabbling, consulting even, occasionally.

Ana winked at Rhys as he walked back into the room with the coffees. His smile told her that he'd heard it all.

Turning to her friend, Ana took her hand. "Tell me everything."

Sins in the Sand

Excerpt

Chapter One

Kendra sighed but kept the practiced smile fixed on her lips. "I'm sorry, but—"

"Sorry is not a word you should use with a patron." The overly starched man glared down his nose at her. "I was told this was a first-class hotel. You should be able to get me whatever I need!" He slammed his hand against the glossy marble of the strategically placed barrier between them.

"Sir..." How could she put this delicately? "We do not procure...that sort of thing." Kendra fought not to shrink away from his wide-eyed rage. She also caught the tremble in his hand and the sweat building at his temples and on his upper lip. Would he turn violent if she couldn't get him what she wanted?

"Where's your manager?" he roared.

"Sir—"

He lunged over the barrier at her. "If you 'sir' me one more time...!"

"Mr. Castillo. What a pleasure to see you again." Julia Monroe slipped in front of Kendra with an easy smile. "How can I help you? I'm Julia, the manager here."

"Your receptionist," he spat, "doesn't seem to understand how to treat guests with the proper respect."

"Kendra is new. I'm sure we can help if you follow me." Julia glanced pointedly at Kendra as she brushed past. She was going to get it when Julia was done with the man.

Still, it was preferable to dealing with an irate, entitled junkie. Forcing her shaking hands to function, she finished off the clerical work she had to do before another patron greeted her.

Being an employee at a Totally Five Star Hotel was an amazing opportunity. Kendra had imagined rubbing shoulders with the rich and famous while working in the most luxurious of hotels. So when she got transferred to Dubai, she thanked her lucky stars. In her mind, she had made it into the best of the best.

It had only been a few weeks, but Kendra had already seen more wonderful and bizarre things than she'd ever wanted and had to deal with some of the most insane clientele imaginable. It ranged from strange requests like taking toy poodles out to relieve themselves — only on real grass — in the middle of the night, to arranging 'private parties' with arrays of women who were obviously paid to be there. And she did it all with a smile.

Rich people were crazy.

She had worked her fingers to the bone while at university to pay her way only to have her father fall ill. It had taken everything she'd earned and then some to make sure he was comfortable in the end. Kendra hadn't finished school, but had managed to get her foot in the door with Totally Five Star. Everyone knew that they took care of their staff.

She'd be set.

If she didn't get herself fired.

After receiving another set of guests, Kendra smoothed her skirt and walked into the break room for a glass of water. It was the first moment she'd had to breathe since getting in that morning. There was a tray of fruit that the staff was allowed to share and sandwiches prepared by one of the hotel's restaurants on top of all the gourmet coffee they could drink, but she had a shake in the fridge that she liked to take sips from whenever she got the chance. It filled her up and kept her going even through the most demanding days.

Kendra opened the fridge, relishing the thought of having some of the shake. Only it wasn't there.

One of the porters walked in as she let the door swing shut. "Ahmed? Do you know if anyone took my shake?"

He shook his head as he straightened his uniform. "I haven't seen a thing." Ahmed stretched his neck from side to side. "I've been running around trying to catch the tiny rat dogs that old lady who came in last night brought with her. Man, those things are fast."

Kendra felt sorry for him. She might have had to deal with some crazy stuff, but Ahmed and the rest of the porters were used like serfs by the clients a lot of the time. "I feel your pain."

He practically inhaled an apple then pounded a soft drink. He sighed happily once it was drained. "Back to work. See you later."

She waved and plucked a few grapes from the tray.

"What are you pouting about now?" Desiree, the other receptionist, sashayed into the room on her Louboutins and sniffed at Kendra disdainfully as she pulled out a bottle of water then took a delicate sip.

"I'm not pouting. And if I was, it would be over someone taking my shake from the fridge."

Desiree screwed up her face. "Why would anyone steal that swill?" She tapped a French-manicured nail against her perfectly painted lips. "Now that you mention it, I did throw out a molding bottle of something this morning."

She nodded toward the garbage.

That conniving… Kendra looked inside to see her still-full bottle sitting in the midst of the trash.

She fished it out and dropped it in the sink.

"I didn't know *that* was still good. It doesn't look fit for anyone to consume. Sorry." She smirked and walked back out.

"Sorry my ass." The woman had had it in for her since the moment she arrived and Kendra had no idea why. They'd never known each other prior to coming to work there. They had been relocated at about the same time — Desiree from Paris and Kendra from Vancouver. They rarely spoke and hardly had anything to do with each other at work and yet, Desiree seemed to hate her.

There was nothing direct or overt. Usually it was a snide comment or a backhanded compliment here and there. Or when they were stuck together, things would just go wrong for Kendra and she knew in her gut that it was because of that woman.

She poured the ruined contents of the bottle down the sink. So much for that. Kendra put the bottle in her little locker and sighed. It was going to be a long night.

Just as she was about to return to her station, Julia strode in with her phone pinned between her shoulder and her ear as she flipped through files on her tablet.

"Yes, it's all been sorted, Katherine. Everything is a go for tomorrow." She sighed. "All right. See you in the morning."

Kendra handed her a bottled water. "It looks like you could use one of these."

Julia took it, twisted the top open with a crack and took a long swig. "Thanks."

"Thank you for dealing with that man earlier." Kendra gave her a half-smile. "I should get back to the desk."

"Desiree can handle that for the moment." Julia took another sip. "Don't let people like that man earlier get you frazzled. You held your own for a while there, which was good. But if you're faced with something that makes you uncomfortable, pass it on to someone else. Just do it discreetly and with a smile — always with a smile."

"I'm not used to that type of demand. He just caught me off guard."

Julia smiled understandingly. "You'll get the hang of it. Quickly," she added.

Kendra certainly hoped so. "I didn't mean to eavesdrop but am I right in thinking that Ms. Murray will be in for tomorrow night's festivities?"

Julia rolled her beautiful brown eyes. "Yes. I guess we should be happy that she hasn't been here since the moment the auction was announced. It's such a big deal I never thought she would leave it to me to handle."

It was a huge undertaking. "I guess she has faith in you."

"More like she can't be everywhere at once." Julia finished off the water and put the bottle in the recycling bin. "But we'll be graced with her presence in the morning while she makes sure everything is up to standard."

Wouldn't that be fun? "I'll get back to the desk now."

Julia nodded as she answered another call.

Kendra was so glad she didn't have to deal with what Julia had to. She'd never been so pleased that she was just a receptionist.

As she walked back out, there was an ear-piercing shriek.

"Kiki Bryant!"

Kendra blinked as an over-bleached and overly tan woman teetered on her heels toward her. "Sorry, I'm not Kiki. My name is Kendra. I'm a receptionist here at the hotel. She should be here in the morning, however."

"Well, that's a disappointment." The blonde scowled. "You look just like her. Though, I would expect the real Kiki Bryant to be dressed a little better." She gave her a once-over and cocked her head critically.

Kendra fought to keep the smile on her face. Her clothes might be functional, but they were among the finest things she'd ever owned. Not that she owned that many clothes.

"I'm sure Ms. Bryant will dazzle you with her style

tomorrow night at the auction."

More books from
Totally Bound Publishing

Part of the Totally 5 Star collection

Can a blackmailing billionaire thaw the heart of an ice princess?

Part of the Totally 5 Star collection

Thou shalt not attack thy Dom — especially not with his own cane.

Part of the Totally 5 Star collection

An ordinary girl catapulted into an extraordinary world meets two even more extraordinary men — but what will she do when she discovers their sexy secret?

Part of the Totally 5 Star collection

Can Tanvi alter kismet's path?

About the Author

Kait Gamble

Kait was born and raised in the wilderness of the Pacific Northwest and started writing to entertain herself during the long winters as a child. Insatiably curious with a love of learning new things, she's picked up many random skills including three languages and two martial arts. After travelling three continents (the other four are on her bucket list), she settled in England with her family where she spends most of her time cultivating her daughter's love of reading and writing, scribbling ideas on every available scrap of paper, and trying out dialogue on her cat.

Kait Gamble loves to hear from readers. You can find contact information, website details and an author profile page at https://www.totallybound.com/

Home of Erotic Romance